OUT WITH THE SUNSET

OUT WITH THE SUNSET

PARKS PAT MYSTERIES #1

P.D. WORKMAN

ISBN: 9781774680612 (IS Hardcover)

ISBN: 9781774680605 (IS Paperback)

ISBN: 9781774680629 (IS Large Print)

ISBN: 9781774680575 (KDP Paperback)

ISBN: 9781774680582 (Kindle)

ISBN: 9781774680599 (ePub)

pdworkman

AND MORE AT PDWORKMAN.COM

To the survivors
Strength and peace

STYLE NOTE

Since my largest readership is in the USA, I have chosen to use US spellings throughout this series. That includes the Americanization of centre to center, even where it is an actual place name, just for consistency's sake. I apologize to my Canadian readers for this.

I have chosen, however, to use Canadian grammar, particularly for Canadian voices. If you see what you think is a grammar error, it may just be Canadian, eh?

CONTENT

Contains discussion of Canadian Residential Schools and other other institutional abuses of children. There are no graphic depictions of violence against children or others, but some readers may be sensitive to these topics.

*M*om, you've got to be kidding me! Are you serious?" Margie winced at Christina's complaint. Up until her phone ringer had shattered their quiet morning preparations, the day had been going well. Bright sunshine streamed in through the kitchen windows of the small house. The rich odor of brewing coffee filled the air. Christina had been blow-drying her long black hair, the hum of the dryer providing a soothing white-noise background as Margie prepared her breakfast and reviewed the day's plans. Everything had been peaceful despite both of their 'first-day' anxieties.

"I know, honey. I didn't plan this. You know I was going to take you to school today and help with your schedule and getting settled in. But…" She gave a dramatic shrug and grimace, "you know I can't control when someone gets murdered."

"Couldn't someone else take this one? You *promised* me."

"They need me. Others in the department will be involved, but this is my first lead, and I can't turn it down."

"You could."

Margie took a deep breath in. Her stomach felt hollow and heavy. She knew she had promised Christina that she would be there for her first day of school. It wasn't fair to expect her to do everything by herself while Margie went off to a murder scene. She was brand new in the Calgary homicide department, and her coworkers would be watching to see how she took on her first case —watching for her to make a mistake. To see whether she was competent, or was just a 'diversity hire' for a department that needed Indigenous representation on the team.

Christina was right, of course; she could turn it down and ask them to make someone else the primary. But what message would that send to the rest of her team about her commitment and ability to handle both her personal life and the rigors of the job?

"Maybe you could start tomorrow instead," Margie suggested. "I could call the school and let them know that you won't be starting today, but you'll be there tomorrow."

"No way!" Christina's response was immediate and emphatic. "I'm starting the same day as everyone else. It's bad enough that I'm the new girl; I'm not going to have everybody looking at me because I didn't start the same day as everyone else. Like I've got some kind of… privilege."

Like Margie's, Christina's black hair, bronze skin, and facial features showed her Cree heritage clearly. Neither one would ever be mistaken for white. But others often saw Indigenous people as lazy, looking for a handout, or expecting compensation for what had happened to them over the generations. Christina wouldn't want to be branded as one of *those Indians*.

"Well, those are the only two options." Margie looked at her watch. "I need to get to the scene. You can go today and get your guidance counselor to help you get everything set up, or you can wait until tomorrow when I can go with you."

Christina slammed the door to the bathroom and started the water running so that Margie couldn't talk to her.

Margie swept her long hair back with both hands and divided it into sections. She deftly braided it and pinned it up into a bun so that it would be neat and out of the way. The coffee machine finished brewing and she poured her coffee into a travel mug.

After making sure she had everything else she would need,

including Staff Sergeant MacDonald's directions to get to the site, she knocked on the bathroom door. "I'm going now. Are you okay?"

"I'm fine," Christina snapped. What she said after that wasn't as easy to make out, but it was something along the lines of "Not that you'd care."

Margie sighed. "Love you, sweetie. I'll see you after school. Give me a call if I'm not home and let me know how your day went."

"You're really going to go take this case and make me go to a new school all by myself?"

"I'm sorry. I can't do anything about it."

Christina slammed something down on the bathroom counter. Margie knew there wasn't anything else she could do or say to smooth things over. Christina was old enough that she could manage. She wasn't a shy or anxious child. She was a strong young woman. She would be able to navigate a new school. Margie had actually been surprised that Christina had wanted her to be there. Usually, she was embarrassed by her mother and didn't want her anywhere close to her teenager peers.

"Goodbye. Love you."

There was no answer from her daughter.

Margie picked up her coffee and her shoulder bag and got into the car. She stuck the note with Sergeant MacDonald's instructions on the dash. After starting the car, she waited for the GPS to boot up. She put Fish Creek Park into the GPS, but the route it popped up was nothing like the directions she had been given. She studied the picture on the small screen. The green area was massive, covering many blocks. So there was undoubtedly more than one entrance. She would have to go by MacDonald's instructions and hope that they were detailed enough to get her there.

She pulled out of the gravel parking pad in the back of the house and found her way out to Twenty-Sixth Street. There was a long multiuse path along the ridge above the irrigation canal, or 'the ditch' as it was known as in the neighborhood. There were always people walking dogs, running, or biking along it. Even late at night or early in the morning, she could almost always count on seeing people on the pathway. She was looking forward to taking Stella out to explore and meet other fur-babies. In September, the trees were still green, with just occasional yellow leaves fluttering to the ground, and there were a lot of parks and green spaces throughout the city. The grass along the path was more yellow than it was green. She hadn't realized before moving to Calgary how arid the city was. The summer temperatures were nothing like they were in Manitoba, but it was still hot and dry. She had thought that it would be a lot more temperate in the shadow of the Rockies.

She found her way to Deerfoot Trail and kept one eye on MacDonald's instructions to make sure that she didn't miss any exits or turns.

Despite the traffic, she pulled into the east entrance to Fish Creek Park in under twenty minutes. There had been no need for lights and siren. The man wasn't going to get any more dead.

CHAPTER TWO

There were more cars in the parking lot than Margie would have expected, and she wondered how many of them could be associated with the investigation and how many were typically there every weekday morning, like the walkers on the path along Twenty-Sixth Street. She supposed that if she lived close to a big park like Fish Creek, she would try to get over there as often as possible. She pulled on a face mask, got out of her car and looked around, trying to figure out which way to go. MacDonald had only given her directions to the parking lot; he hadn't told her where to go from there. She had hoped to be able to see the crime scene from there, but all she saw were trees.

"Detective Pat—er—Patter..." A man in a gray uniform shirt, dark pants, and gun belt approached her with his hand outstretched. He had a bandana-style mask.

Margie reached automatically to shake, then drew back and gave him a little wave. "Patenaude," she told him, pronouncing it clearly for him, "PAT-en-ode."

"Oh, that's not so hard." He gave an embarrassed laugh. He dropped his hand to his side. "French?"

"Yes. Métis."

"Sure." He gestured toward her face, indicating her dark skin and whatever he could see of her nose and other features above the mask. "I should have guessed. We don't see a lot of Natives in law enforcement. Sorry."

Margie shrugged it off. "I guess if you know my name, you know what I'm here for."

"Yes," he seemed far more comfortable with this topic. "You're here for our body."

He said it possessively, maybe even a little affectionately. *Our body.* She glanced at his gray uniform. Not the black shirt of a Calgary Police Services uniform. "What department are you with?"

"Alberta Parks. I'm one of the Conservation Officers here. Dave Barnes."

"Okay." Margie nodded. "You know the park well, then."

"Very well. Come on; I'll take you to the crime scene."

She followed him to an electric golf cart and took the passenger seat. Margie looked around her as Barnes drove down one of the bicycle paths, slowing and occasionally tapping his horn as they passed cyclists out for a morning ride.

"The park looked pretty big on my GPS screen. How big is it?"

"Thirteen and a half square kilometers with ninety kilometers of trails."

"Whoa. I'm glad you've got a cart."

"Me too. But we don't have too far to go today. We're just headed to Hull's Wood."

Margie watched the sunlight filtering through the green leaves, creating dappled shadows on the pavement of the pathway. It all seemed so peaceful and idyllic, people walking and running, some with dogs or companions and some alone, the occasional bicycles thrumming along beside them. A paradise in the middle of the busy city. She had been impressed by Calgary's long list of parks, both city and provincial. She liked to walk and bike. She was hoping to be able to ride her bike to work, taking the new bridge alongside Blackfoot Trail, then through

Pearce Estate Park and along the Bow River Pathway to get downtown. It would be much better for her than always driving her car. Once she got settled in and more familiar with the route.

"Here we are." Barnes's words drew her attention back to the present and to the not-so-idyllic scene she was there to see.

Tape had been looped around several trees to cordon off the area. Sunlight streamed down on a small clearing. Bright green grass against the dark trunks of the trees. The grass and wild plants had a fresh, sweet scent. There were more gray-shirted conservation officers and a few dark-uniformed Calgary Police officers hanging around. A crime scene truck was parked outside the cordoned area, waiting for Margie to review the scene and give them the go-ahead to collect forensic evidence.

She dismounted from the cart and looked slowly around before advancing to the crime scene. She looked at the spectators rubbernecking nearby, all hoping to catch a glimpse of something exciting or disgusting to brag about to their friends and family.

No one who seemed out of place. No one who appeared to be anything other than curious as to what had happened. But one never knew. Sometimes killers returned to the scene or stayed around to watch the discovery and investigation go down.

Margie approached the crime scene truck and nodded at the techs who were suited up, face shields on and ready to go.

"Hi. I'm Detective Patenaude. New in town. You guys been here long?"

A couple held disposable cups of Tim's coffee, looking like they had been waiting for her for a while.

"Half hour," one of them commented, thumbing his phone to check the time.

"Okay. Sorry to keep you waiting." Margie pulled on her own protective gear, trying not to fumble or look incompetent in front of them. It wasn't her first rodeo and she didn't want them thinking that she was inexperienced. "While I take a look, do you think you could get pictures of the bystanders?"

One of the men holding a Tim's cup raised an eyebrow. "The bystanders?"

"Yeah. If you could just do that sort of unobtrusively, so we've got a record if one of them ends up being a witness or suspect?"

Most of the observers were not wearing masks, which was lucky. One of the unfortunate effects of mandatory masking policies was the increased difficulty of reading and recognizing faces.

The tech exchanged a look with his coworkers, then shrugged and nodded. "Pictures of the bystanders. Roger."

"Thanks." Margie finished with her protective gear and lifted one of the lines of tape to duck under it. She made her way over to the body with great care, watching for any footprints or crushed vegetation.

One of the uniformed cops nodded to her. He wasn't masked and kept his distance. He had a medium build and a round face, hair thinning on top. "You the primary?" he asked.

"Yes. Hope I didn't keep you waiting too long."

"He might have gotten a degree or two colder while we were waiting, but it's not like he's going to get up and walk away."

Margie chuckled. "No," she agreed. She looked at his name bar. "Officer Smith. You want to walk me through it?"

"Found by a dog walker this morning. As you can see," he tilted his head toward the spectators on the pathway, "there is a lot of foot traffic here, even very early in the morning. Dogs are really good at smelling out bodies. The riper, the better."

"But this one hasn't been here very long," Margie observed. The body hadn't been there long enough for her to detect any decomp.

She gazed down at the crumpled figure. Looked like a male, but he was face-down, so she wouldn't be able to verify until he had been moved. Tall and slim. He seemed deflated beneath the wrinkled jacket and pants. The vegetation in the area had not been trampled down; Margie couldn't see any sign of a major struggle. And there was not a lot of blood and gore. Most of that would be underneath him.

"Has anyone touched him? Moved him?"

"Just to verify that he didn't have a pulse and check for signs of violence."

Margie raised her brows questioningly.

"Stabbed," Smith informed her. "Center mass. Probably too low for the heart, but could have punctured a lung or caught the aorta. Not just a heart attack on his morning constitutional."

Margie stooped briefly to feel for a pulse—never hurt to have it verified more than once—and to evaluate the temperature and rigidity of the body. Someone from the medical examiner's office would be there to take the liver temp and make other observations, such as rigor, but Margie wanted to know for herself as she began the investigation.

"He's been here a while," she observed. "I don't think it happened this morning. More likely last night."

Smith didn't disagree. "The park closes at night. But that doesn't mean someone didn't stick around and avoid being seen. A place like this, you can't check behind every rock. The CO's do what they can to keep anyone from setting up camp here, but still come across homeless encampments now and then hidden in the bush. It's a big park."

Margie looked around. "I guess we don't have the luxury of surveillance cameras like we would if this happened on the street."

"Actually, there are some. I don't know where they all are."

"Probably the parking lots."

"There are wildlife cams too, though. And some of the trails are probably monitored. You can ask the CO's what video they have. Maybe you'll get lucky."

"Not lucky enough to have a video of the actual murder," Margie posited. "That would be too much to expect."

Smith shrugged. "Yeah. You're probably right."

Margie looked around at the ground for anything that was out of place. "Is the knife still in him? If not, did you take a look around for it?"

"Not in him. I kept my eyes open while we were deciding how

much area to rope off. I was hoping it might have been dropped close by. But we didn't see anything. We can take another look, now that it's daylight. It was still pretty dark when we got here."

Sunrise had been around seven o'clock the last few days, Margie knew. Of course there had been runners and dog walkers out before that. People trying to get their workouts in before heading to office or retail jobs starting at eight or nine.

So when was their victim killed? During the small hours of the morning before opening? Or late at night when he shouldn't have even been in the park? She hoped they would be able to narrow it down quickly.

"Did you get all of the contact information for the dog walker who found him? And what about him, did he touch the body?"

"Dog might have contaminated it. Owner kept his distance after bringing the dog under control. We got everything we needed from him, down to the dog's name and morning routine. You can give him a call and talk to him or request an interview any time today. He's eager to help."

"Great. Thanks. Do we have an identity for our victim yet?"

"Haven't searched him. He's fully dressed—you know, not for running or something—so he probably has a wallet on him, unless it was a robbery. We figured we'd let the techies do that part."

Margie nodded. It was a good call. They might even have a missing person report on him already if he had a family and should have been home the night before.

She looked around some more without moving her feet, but couldn't see any other clues and didn't want to be guilty of contaminating the scene any further. She looked toward the crime scene investigators and nodded to them.

"Let's get out of the way and let them do their thing," she advised Smith, raising her voice a little for everyone within the cordoned-off area.

CHAPTER THREE

While Margie got out of the way to allow the crime scene techs to do their job, she wandered casually toward the bystanders. She wasn't wearing a uniform but, of course, it would be apparent to everyone there that she was a police detective. They wouldn't have allowed just anyone to get that close to the body. But no one peeled abruptly away from the group or attracted her attention.

"My name is Detective Marguerite Patenaude," she told the onlookers in a friendly, pleasant tone. "I wonder if anyone here happened to see anything this morning? Not necessarily him," she motioned back toward the body, "but anything that's out of the ordinary for the park. Most of you probably walk or run here several times a week?"

Most of them nodded automatically. A few looked away. Maybe they had just been called by their friends to come to see what was going on, in hopes of being able to see something brag-worthy.

"So? Anything unusual? People or activities that you don't normally see? A strange noise or smell? Anything that made you take notice?"

No one stepped forward to offer anything. Most shook their

heads and made negative noises. Margie hadn't actually expected to get anything from them. More than likely, the murder had happened many hours before, and the people who walked the park in the morning were not the same ones who walked it in the evening.

"Anybody want my card? In case you think of something or hear anything from someone else?" Margie pulled a stack of business cards out of her pocket and held them out, offering them to each person. A couple people took one. Maybe hoping she'd be able to help them out of a speeding ticket at some point. No one met her eyes or gave her the impression that they would call her later when they could speak to her without witnesses. "All right. Thank you. You can move along, you can't see much from here, and we'll be around for a while. You might as well finish your workouts."

Most of them moved on. Only a few lingered. None of them did anything to make her think that they might know what had happened. No one started asking her questions about the murder. There was no one who appeared to be from the press, though she was sure they would be there within the hour. Even if there were nothing to report, they still had to get some shots at the scene and report that there was nothing to report.

Before long, a couple of the other homicide detectives from Margie's team made it to the site. Margie tried to remember their names and what she knew about them. She'd only had one brief meeting with the team so far, when she had been introduced to them and read in on all of the usual policies and procedures. She had filled out her tax forms and been assigned a desk and told when she would be on duty. Even though she had known she would be on duty on Christina's first day, she had made arrangements not to be at the office until later in the day once she got Christina settled at the school. None of them had anticipated that they would be called to a homicide early that morning. That was just the way that it went. You couldn't plan.

Detective Cruz would have played a good Hispanic cop on TV. Olive skin, hair turning to salt and pepper, a short mustache now hidden behind a mask, and a bit of a paunch. But he'd made it clear when they met that he was Filipino, not Hispanic. Margie had been surprised to find such a large Filipino community in Calgary. She had thought Calgary's demographics would skew a lot more white—and redneck—but there was a surprisingly multi-cultural population. Half of the people in her neighborhood seemed to be either Asian or Polynesian. Cruz was an older cop, probably ready for retirement before too long. Homicide was not an easy job. People didn't stay there for more than two or three years, and Cruz had been there at least four.

Riding with Cruz was Detective Kaitlyn Jones. Margie had been happy to discover that she would not to be the sole woman on the homicide team. She could hold her own; she'd always been able to fit in as "one of the guys," but it was still a relief to know that there was another woman there who would have her back in case of any sexist or harassing behavior. Boys would be boys, but she was not going to put up with any garbage.

Margie filled them in on her arrival on the scene and every-thing they had done before Cruz and Jones arrived.

"The victim did have a wallet. It gives his name as Jerry Robinson, and his face matches the picture on his ID." She read off the address from his driver's license. "I guess that's not far from here?"

"Deer Run," Cruz said with a nod. "Not far at all. Might have walked in."

"The CO's haven't seen any abandoned vehicles, anything left overnight, so he probably did."

"Any background on him yet?" Jones asked. Her blond hair was pulled back into a bun, and despite the blue mask over her face, Margie could still tell by the cheer in her voice and the fan of laugh lines around her eyes she was smiling. "Wedding ring? Business card? Family pictures?"

Margie laid out what they had. "Union card; apparently he is a welder. Don't know about family or kids yet; his phone is locked. No wedding ring, but that might just be so he doesn't injure himself on a job site. We'll have to do some background and find out if he has a family, make a death notification to the next of kin. I haven't checked social media yet, but that might be a good place to start."

"So it wasn't robbery," Cruz mused. "Everything appeared to be in his wallet? Cash? Plastic? Jewelry wasn't stolen?"

"Doesn't look like robbery. He could have had a watch or necklace or something of value, but we won't know that until we talk to people who knew him. There's no mark on his finger showing that he typically wears a ring, but he could still have one and only wear it some of the time. Cash and credit cards in his wallet. Not a lot, but if the motive had been robbery, I would have expected at least the cash to disappear."

"Okay. Makes sense. Any sign he's been in a fight?"

"We'll have to wait for the ME's report, but nothing obvious. Hands are scarred from working. No split knuckles or broken nose."

"Then what happened?" Jones asked, shaking her head. "Usually, it's pretty obvious. Robbery, fight, drug or gang connection. In a park like this, at night, it could be drugs, but…?"

But Margie hadn't mentioned anything that would give them that idea. "Nothing that I could see. The body certainly doesn't scream drug dealer or addict."

CHAPTER FOUR

*I*nvestigating even a major crime like homicide, there was a lot of 'hurry up and wait.' They would have to wait for the video surveillance. For the medical examiner's report. For the techs to crack the code on Robinson's phone if he didn't have a family member who knew it.

By the time they got to the duty room, it was already midafternoon. Phones rang, people banged away at their keyboards and chatted with each other in voices that were a little too loud for Margie to concentrate. Her desk was out in the bullpen, not behind a closed door, and she found it a little distracting.

And she had promised Christina that she would get home early.

"It's my daughter's first day of school," Margie told Jones, hoping she would be the most sympathetic. "Would you mind screening Robinson to see if we have anything on him or if you can find him on social media, and I'll check in with you later? I'd like to pick her up at school or at least take her out for a burger once she gets home. I had promised to go in with her this morning and then I couldn't."

"Sure," Jones agreed. "How old is your daughter?"

"She's fifteen—a terrible age to uproot her and come to Calgary, her first year in high school. I mean, she was in high school last year, but grade nine was high school in Winnipeg, and the high school here starts at grade ten. So even though she had her first year of high school in Winnipeg last year, she's the little fish again this year. In a new school. In a new city."

"That's tough," Jones agreed. "Which school?"

"Forest Lawn High."

"Oh."

Margie tried to interpret Jones's reaction. She didn't immediately tell Margie what a great school it was, even though the principal had really talked up the school and its programs. But it wasn't like she had badmouthed it either. Maybe she or a friend had gone there for high school.

"Where did you go?"

"Oh, I wasn't in Calgary during high school. Ft. McMurray."

Northern Alberta. Where the tar sands were. Margie nodded. "Cold there?"

Jones shuddered. "Oh yes, it was. No Chinooks there."

"I'm looking forward to experiencing a Chinook wind. We don't get them in Winnipeg. Once it gets cold there, it stays cold all winter."

"One of the best things about Calgary," Jones agreed. "Though it wreaks havoc with the roads. And sometimes the trees, if they think it is spring before it is. And migraine headaches."

Margie nodded, her attention no longer on the subject. She gathered her things. "You have my cell number in case you need to reach me? Sorry to be ducking out early on my first homicide, but I'll be in bright and early in the morning, and you can reach me tonight if you need me."

"Go take care of your daughter. We'll be fine."

MARGIE DIDN'T QUITE MAKE it in time to pick Christina up from school, so she hurried back to the house instead to beat her there and try to smooth things out for when she arrived. She let Stella out to run in the yard for a few minutes, tidied up the living room and kitchen, and tried to decide what they would do for supper. She didn't call or text Christina while she was on the bus, which would probably just irritate her. And she didn't want to inundate her daughter with questions as soon as she got in the door. But she also didn't want to look like she had just been home relaxing while Christina dealt with school and the bus ride home.

Eventually, Christina got home. Later than Margie had expected. Maybe she should have gone to the school to pick her up after all. Christina pushed the door open with a loud bang, then stepped in and slammed it behind her. She ripped off her mask.

Margie kept her temper. Of course Christina was tired and irritable after a long day at school, and she wanted to show her displeasure with her mother for letting her down. Margie forced a welcoming smile. "Hi, honey. How was it?"

If looks could kill, she would have had to arrest her own daughter for murder. Or one of the other homicide detectives would have to, since Margie herself would have been dead. Christina dropped her backpack on the floor and flounced down onto the couch.

"Was it that bad? I'm so sorry. Tell me all about it."

"We should have stayed in the Peg. I don't understand why we had to come here. Your job there was just fine, and I had friends and knew my way around the school and the bus system and everything else there. We should have just stayed. Couldn't we have stayed until I was done school? Three more years? Would that have been so bad? Then you could go wherever you wanted to, and I could go to university or start working. Why did we have to come here?"

Christina was one of the reasons that Margie had wanted to move away from Winnipeg. Yes, Christina had friends there and knew her way around, but that was part of the problem. Margie hadn't liked Christina's friends, and there was a lot of violence and drug culture in Winnipeg. As a cop, Margie knew the statistics about murdered or missing Indigenous women in the Peg. She hadn't wanted Christina to become another statistic.

"What happened?" she persisted. "Did something bad happen, or is it just because it is difficult getting used to a new place?"

"I hate it. Why did you move us to the hood? We had a nice place in Winnipeg. Here, we're in the ghetto!" She kicked at her schoolbag with a thud.

"Ghetto? Calgary doesn't have a ghetto or a hood. This is a nice area. Lots of families and retired couples that have been here for years."

"It's the *hood*. That's what the kids at school say. Forest Lawn is the hood, and everybody who goes to the school is in a gang."

"We aren't in Forest Lawn. We're in Southview. And I checked out the crime statistics before we came. It isn't bad. There is crime all over; you can't escape that. There isn't a lot of gang activity at the school. Maybe some kids there are in gangs, but that was true in Winnipeg too. The crime rate there was *much* higher than here. I don't think you need to worry that you've been dumped into the middle of a war zone."

Christina shook her head irritably. "I should have known you wouldn't listen."

"I am listening." Margie tried to tone it down. Christina needed to know she was being heard; she didn't need her mother arguing statistics. "Tell me more about it. I'll try to keep my mouth shut and just listen to you. I didn't mean to argue. Did you make any friends? Meet anyone interesting?"

"At home, everybody was First Nations or Métis. It's different here. Everybody is white. Or Asian. Or Black. There aren't that many Indigenous kids."

Margie nodded. "I know. The demographics are a bit different. Calgary has lots of immigrants."

"So I'm, like, I stand out. I look Cree, so everyone thinks that

I'm… I don't know. Just there for a free ride, or drugs, or to steal their stuff. They look at me like I'm…" Christina shook her head, at a loss for words. "I don't know. Like I'm dirty or a criminal."

Christina threw her head back against the back of the couch in frustration.

"Oh, honey." Margie hoped that Christina was just overre-acting and being dramatic. She had found so far that Calgarians treated her pretty well. But she was an adult with tough skin and a badge. Not a sensitive teenager. "I'm sorry you felt so much like an outsider."

Christina nodded vigorously. "Exactly. Like an outsider. I hate it. I just want to go home."

"Is there any way I can help? We're not moving back to Winnipeg, but is there anything else I can do to help make it better?"

"The school is huge. I'm so lost. And everybody already has friends. I don't have anybody."

"Give it a few days. I'm sure other people are new, and people who are looking for new friends. They'll be coming from all different junior highs, so everyone will have to meet new people, and friendships will be changing. Maybe we could look at some clubs or after-school activities that will help you get in with a group sooner."

"I don't want to do sports or photography or any other stupid hobbies. I want to… hang out with friends like I did in Winnipeg."

One of the things that Margie hadn't liked in Winnipeg was how much unsupervised time Christina and her friends had for hanging around, looking for new ways to get in trouble.

"I'm going to be connecting with the Métis community here. I'm sure you'll be able to make some friends through the Métis Nation or Friendship Center so you won't feel so different."

Christina shrugged. It wasn't an objection, so it felt like a win —score one for Mom.

"And when we visit Moushoom, we can see if he has some

other suggestions. There are probably cousins we don't even know about here. Not as many as at home—in Winnipeg—but you might be able to connect with someone."

Christina's head went up. "When are we going to go see Moushoom? That's one of the reasons you said we should move here. Well, we're here, so when are we going to go see him?"

Margie didn't even have all of their boxes unpacked. But she was glad that Christina wanted to see her great-grandfather. Other kids might roll their eyes and say they didn't want to visit some old person in a nursing home. Though it wasn't a nursing home. It was an independent living facility. Margie and some of the cousins had been worried about his still living on his own. It was hard to tell from so far away whether he still had all of his faculties or whether he should have more care and supervision. Someone looking after him and making sure he took his pills and ate what he should.

"I was going to suggest that we go out for burgers to celebrate your first day of school and my first homicide. Or… commiserate. I don't suppose 'celebrate' is the right word."

"Yeah? And then go see Moushoom? Maybe we could take him a burger; I bet he would like that."

Margie hesitated. "I don't know if he is on a special diet. We'd better find that out before we take him any food. But we could get some supper and then go see him afterwards."

Christina nodded her approval at this. "Where are we going to go?"

"I don't really know what's good. There are a ton of ethnic restaurants on Seventeenth Avenue. They call it International Avenue. But if we're going to go see Moushoom, maybe we should just get something quick, so we're not stuck waiting for an hour for our food. There's an A&W. You like their burgers."

"Do they have a veggie burger?"

Margie frowned at her. "A veggie burger? Maybe, I don't know."

"I decided I want to be vegetarian."

That was a bit of a shock. Christina had always enjoyed her meat. And even hunting. Margie hadn't seen that one coming. Her brain immediately spun into high gear. Was Christina flirting with an eating disorder? Looking for ways to cut her food intake or calories? Would she be able to get the protein she needed on a vegetarian diet? Teen girls needed plenty of iron if they didn't want to be anemic.

But she answered as calmly as she could. It was probably just a passing phase. This week, Christina would be vegetarian, and next week, she would be ordering a rack of ribs.

"I'm sure they must have a veggie burger." Stella barked from outside the back door, and Margie took a couple of steps toward it to let her in. "Why don't you look it up on your phone and make sure they have what you want? Then we can head over."

She opened the door and let Stella in. She scratched her floppy ears and cuddled her black and brown face, asking, 'Who's a good girl?' Then Stella noticed that Christina was home and launched herself at her. Christina squealed and laughed and wrestled with Stella. Margie smiled at the two of them. Stella was good therapy at the end of a rough day.

A&W did have a veggie burger, and it was pretty good. Christina gave Margie a bite and, despite her hesitation, Margie found that it tasted pretty much just like a regular beef burger. This made her wonder how much beef was in a regular beef burger and how much was fillers of some kind. You wanted breadcrumbs or something to help give it a good texture and moisture, but not too much.

"That's great," Margie observed. "Maybe I'll get one next time." She nearly patted her stomach and commented on getting too thick around the middle, but stopped herself. She didn't want Christina to start worrying about her weight or to model her own thoughts about her body after negative comments her mother made.

Christina finished her burger in a few more bites and dabbled some remaining fries in the puddle of ketchup. "Where does Moushoom live? Is it far away?"

Calgary was the big city. Not like the population of New York, of course, but it was bigger than Winnipeg, and it sprawled over hundreds of square kilometers. It could take an hour to drive across the city. Margie smiled. "He's very close. We'll drive over today, but you can walk there from the house. You can go see him any time you want."

Christina smiled broadly at that. "Really? That's awesome."

She loved her Moushoom. They cleared away their garbage and went back to the car. Margie used the GPS even though she knew it was close. She didn't want to head in the wrong direction. Once she had been there a few times, she would be able to get there without instructions. For a descendant of Cree women and explorers, Margie had a terrible sense of direction.

❧

MARGIE SCANNED the signs on the door to the building. They were, of course, required to wear masks while visiting. There was a hand sanitizing station to wash before going up to the living quarters and upon leaving, to protect both their loved ones and themselves. There was a long list of symptoms. *If you have experienced a new cough, fever, upset stomach, trouble breathing...*

But no unexpected rules. Nothing about having to quarantine for fourteen days if they had come from out of the province. That was a relief. She had been secretly worried about it, even though she had told Christina that she could visit whenever she wanted to. They already had their masks on, so they rubbed gel into their hands and continued on to the elevators.

Moushoom was sitting in an easy chair, watching the TV when they arrived. He hollered for them to come in rather than getting up to answer the door. When he saw they were visitors rather than staff, he sat up straighter.

"Who's there?"

"It's Margie and Christina, Moushoom," Margie informed him. Christina stepped forward to hug him, but Margie touched her to prevent her. "We have to be careful of infection," she reminded.

Christina shook her head. "I'm going to hug him! I'll hold my breath, and I just washed my hands. I'm not going to infect him!"

Moushoom eagerly accepted a hug from Christina. "Is it really little Christina? But you were just a little girl the last time I saw you!"

"That was two summers ago. I... grew up."

"Yes, you did." Moushoom released his hold on her and looked her over. "You are turning into a lovely young lady. Your mother must be very proud."

"Isn't she?" Margie agreed. She drew a couple of chairs over so they could sit close—but not too close—to him. "We have a surprise for you."

"A bigger surprise than this? I didn't think they would even let people travel right now. Everything has been so crazy with the pandemic."

"A bigger surprise than this."

Margie looked at the old man with great affection. He still looked just the same as she remembered him. He wore his buck-skins, beadwork, and sash proudly. He was always reminding them of their heritage. Telling them not to forget their history and where they had come from. It was all important. It wasn't just where they had come from; it was a piece of who they were. Maybe he was a little shrunken, a little more gray than she remembered him, but otherwise, he looked exactly the same. Her own Moushoom.

"What could it be? What is it?"

"We bought a house just a few blocks from here," Christina burst out. "So we can come and visit you all the time."

His eyes widened in surprise and delight. "Are you pulling my leg? How could that be? You lived in…" It took him a minute to dredge it up, "in Winnipeg."

"We did," Margie agreed. "But I got a job with Calgary homicide. And now we live here."

"That's great!" Moushoom enthused. "It will be so great to have you close by!"

CHAPTER FIVE

Margie wasn't thinking that it was so great when she was driving downtown before dawn the next morning to get a head start on her investigation. She felt guilty about having gone home so early the day before, leaving the rest of the team to handle the investigation while she went home to be with her family. No one had complained, but of course they would be watching her to see whether it was a regular thing and whether she was going to take advantage of them. They probably figured that she would have some special privileges, being female and Métis, because if they complained about her, they could be accused of being sexist and racist, of not understanding how difficult things were for her as a single mom and a minority.

She didn't want to reinforce those stereotypes. She had always been a hard worker. She hated to be classified as a 'lazy Indian' and did everything she could to avoid being seen that way, even if it meant putting in more hours and effort than anyone else on the team. Even when it meant driving to work while it was still pitch black outside, with not even a sliver of light on the horizon.

Calgary's cold and changeable weather destroyed the roads, the water seeping into cracks and then expanding when it froze there, widening the gaps even more. It was too difficult to do roadwork when it was thirty below. As the joke went, there were two seasons in Calgary: winter and construction. So Margie avoided the potholes, lost her lanes due to construction pylons and tape, and followed detour signs until she finally made it downtown and pulled into the underground parking. The lighting was dim, but what could be safer than a police parkade? There wouldn't be anyone lurking around there looking to cause trouble.

She sat down at her desk and checked her physical and electronic inboxes to see what had come in the afternoon before or overnight that she could start working on. She saw that videos had been loaded onto the server space for the new case. Lots of video. That was great, possibly giving them a way to narrow down the time of the murder and who had been in the area at that point. And it was also bad because it meant that she would be staring at the screen for a long time, processing hours of videos from various camera feeds.

Detective Siever had sent her an email outlining what video had been uploaded. She tried to remember his face. Middle-aged, round face, buzz cut. He had seemed like a nice guy when they had been introduced.

Camera feed 8302 is the camera closest to the crime scene. Start with that.

Bless you, Detective Siever. Margie started with the video prefaced with 8302. It ran from midday until about the time that Margie had reached the scene. That was what, eighteen hours of video? Margie breathed out slowly, trying to figure out how to approach it. She wasn't going to start at the beginning. Midday was way too early. There would have been a lot of people and dogs through the park at that time. Since the body had not been discovered until early the next morning, she had to assume that Robinson had been killed either shortly before or sometime after the park had closed. Referring to the park's website, she found that to be ten o'clock.

She started at the end of the video and began scrubbing backwards. She watched as all of the emergency responders backed out of the scene and the frame was empty except for a man and a dog. They reversed off the screen. Margie could not see Robinson's body with the distance and angle of the camera location, but she could see approximately where it was. Not right on the pathway, but a ways into the woods. She scrubbed backwards some more, watching for anyone else walking along the pathway or through the camera frame. There was one passerby in the wee hours of the morning, and she stopped and played the video at normal speed to watch a homeless man push a shopping cart loaded high with garbage bags past the camera. He didn't leave the pathway or deviate from his course. Margie made a notation of the time and a short explanation and continued to scrub backwards.

No golf carts. No other homeless people. No sign of Robinson himself. Back, and back, and back, until she crossed the time stamp for ten o'clock. Margie hesitated, wondering if she had missed something. But it was possible that the homicide had occurred before ten o'clock, so she kept going. She started to see the last few stragglers before the park had closed. She froze the video and took screenshots, getting the best pictures she could of the people leaving the park, walking toward the camera. She made notes of the timestamps and quick descriptions of the people. Woman with dog. Couple walking hand-in-hand. Man in hoodie. Cyclist. Skateboarding kid. Then she reached a point in the tape where there were people both coming and going, which made it more complicated. The last few people who had taken their late-evening walks on that pathway. Some of them she recognized because she had already seen them leave. The couple walking hand-in-hand. Skateboarding kid.

Then the victim. Margie watched him walk by the camera. His back was to it so that she couldn't see his face, but he had been wearing a coat. It was getting chilly in the evenings. Down to six degrees lately. She paused the video and searched for the photos taken at the scene to compare the man's attire to Robinson's. It was him, or someone dressed exactly the same way. She noted the time. She now had a much better idea of the time of death. Sometime after eight-thirty. Probably between eight-thirty and ten. Unless the killer was the homeless guy she had seen after ten. There hadn't been anyone else around. Not visible on that camera.

She watched Robinson walk down the path and wander off into the woods. Not taking pictures. Not, as far as she could tell, meeting someone else. Sneaking off to relieve himself? Just enjoying the green trees and lengthening shadows? Going to a favorite clearing to meditate or walking to the edge of the river she had seen when scouting the area earlier?

He didn't come back into sight after disappearing off of the screen. He had been killed out of view of the camera. Margie let the video play forwards, watching each of the people who arrived and left the park after Robinson. Was one of them the killer, or had he managed to avoid cameras? Was it a planned attack? Had the killer scoped out all of the cameras first and then avoided them? She thought about the injury. A single stab in the middle of the body. Not multiple wounds. Not someone who had gone for the throat or had been aiming for the heart. What did that signify? A professional hit? An accident? A lucky shot? It didn't strike her as a crime of passion. Not that a death in the middle of the park sounded like a crime of passion anyway, but she hadn't ruled it out completely.

As the video rolled forward, she made sure that she had noted the arrivals and departures in her list and hadn't missed anyone. She scrutinized the faces she could see. Anyone who was upset? Angry? Overwrought?

She didn't like the people whose faces she could not see. People with masks, baseball caps, the guy with the dark hoodie. She wanted to be able to see their expressions, to be able to identify them if she saw them again. She wanted to compare the faces to those she'd had taken of the bystanders in the morning. Had one of them stuck around to watch what happened once the body was discovered?

"Patenaude. Detective Patenaude. Pat. Hey. Patenaude!"

Margie pulled her focus from the video to the room. People

had arrived without her taking any notice of the fact. Cruz was leaning close, trying to get her attention. When she finally heard him and saw him, Cruz chuckled and shook his head at the rest of the team.

"Now that's focus!"

"Sorry, I was lost in my own little world," Margie apologized.

"We have a morning briefing. You ready?"

"Uh… yeah. Give me just a minute." Margie looked at her watch and then at the papers and notes scattered around her. Morning briefing, and it wouldn't just be MacDonald briefing the team, but Margie briefing him on what they had accomplished so far, sharing progress with the rest of the team, and making assignments. It was one reason she had wanted to get there as early as she could to get a head start on the work she had left incomplete the afternoon before.

"Five minutes," Cruz advised. "And Mac doesn't like people to be late."

"I'll be there."

Margie tried to gather her notes together in some semblance of order. She looked at herself in her phone camera to make sure that she looked presentable.

"Funny time to take a selfie," Jones commented. "You should be getting a move on it."

"Not a selfie. Just making sure I look okay."

"Look fine to me. Let's go." Jones motioned toward the conference room. Margie took a deep breath and preceded Jones into the room. She was momentarily disconcerted by the fact that everyone was standing around the table, no one sitting down. Was this some kind of chivalrous behavior? The men waiting until the women were seated, or showing Margie respect because it was her case or her first briefing? She reached to pull one of the chairs out, and Jones put her hand on Margie's arm.

"No, it's a stand-up meeting."

"A stand-up meeting?" Margie repeated stupidly, trying to process it.

"MacDonald says we think better on our feet. It keeps anyone from falling asleep and ensures that meetings are as quick as they can be."

"Okay, then." Margie put her papers down on the table in front of her and waited, like everyone else, standing around the table.

Staff Sergeant MacDonald entered the room. A tall man with short-cropped gray hair, thin-rimmed glasses, and a deeply lined face. He looked around at the team and nodded briskly. "Let's get to it, then. How are we doing on the Fish Creek Park case?" He consulted his notes. "Jerry Robinson."

Everyone's eyes turned to Margie. She cleared her throat. "We are still waiting for the full postmortem results, but apparent cause of death was a single stab wound to the abdomen. Robbery does not appear to be a motive. No missing person report had been filed and there was no answer when Cruz knocked on his door, so we suspect that he lived alone; no partner or children. I have been going through video. I'm still just beginning my review of the video, but I believe I have identified Robinson entering the area at 8:23 p.m."

There were murmurs from the team.

"If it's him, that helps quite a bit with the time of death."

"Yes. We'll get confirmation from the medical examiner, but I don't think she'll be able to narrow it down any more than that. I've been making notes of everyone else that I can see entering or leaving after Robinson's arrival—looking for any aberrant behaviors, emotion, someone who is running or appears distressed. Nothing so far. I don't see anyone who seems to be out of place or behaving strangely."

"No one covered in blood?" Cruz joked.

Margie shook her head. "Sorry, no. No one covered in blood. No one who seems to be in too much of a hurry. There are not a lot of park-goers there after Robinson, so it isn't a huge pool of suspects, but of course, it's going to take some work to identify them all."

"They're probably mostly regulars," Jones suggested. "If we were to go back there around the same time tonight, we could probably get ID's on a good number on them, and maybe some suggestions on how to find the others from the regulars. These are probably people who are local who use the park all the time."

Margie nodded. "Good idea. You're probably right. We might be able to narrow down the suspects that way—if it was me, and I had killed someone in the park, I probably wouldn't go back there. Not for a while, anyway."

MacDonald gave a nod. "You may be right there. Let's get some people canvassing there tonight. Who is available?"

Margie indicated she was. Christina would be home from school. There would be time for supper and for Christina to get settled in on her homework. She was old enough to be left alone while Margie went back out to canvass the park for a couple of hours looking for witnesses and trying to match faces to names. Most of the rest of the team indicated that they would be able to help. A dedicated bunch. No one complained about not being able to spend the evening with their families or watching the NHL playoffs.

They had a lot of work ahead of them if they were going to crack the case.

CHAPTER SIX

*C*hristina was less angry when she arrived home than she had been the first day of school, but she was still sullen about having to move there and obviously not enjoying the new school yet. Margie had been hoping that she would have made at least one friend, which would help her to get through the first few weeks of school until she started to feel more at home. But apparently, that was not in the cards. Maybe in another day or two, Christina and another new girl would gravitate toward each other, or she would be admitted into one of the already-established circles of friends.

These things took time.

They had a quick meal of tacos made with microwaved beans.

"I'm going to take Stella for a quick walk out on the pathway," Margie told Christina. "Do you want to come with us?"

Christina hesitated. Margie didn't push it. The last thing she needed to do was make Christina think that Margie wanted her to go with her. That would just convince her to shut herself in her room and refuse to go out. Margie stayed casual about it, going to the door to put on her shoes and calling Stella for walkies.

"I guess I can come," Christina said eventually. "I don't have that much homework tonight. It's too early for them to be assigning anything big. They have to figure out where everyone is first. Since people are coming from all different schools," she pointed out.

Margie nodded. "That makes sense," she agreed. "They'll need to do some remedial stuff and to get everyone on the same level first, won't they? At least with some basics."

Christina petted Stella and scratched her soft brown ears before picking up her own shoes. "We should get some moccasins like Moushoom's."

"I don't know how they would fare on the pathways. You wouldn't want them to be ruined."

"They're meant to be worn outside."

Margie nodded. She was glad to see Christina showing some interest in the traditional clothing. She didn't expect Christina to start wearing a sash to school, but she liked that Christina was aware of her culture and felt positive about what she saw Moushoom doing. A lot of kids might have just thought him a funny old man.

Margie clipped on Stella's leash, and they headed out the door. It was only a couple of blocks to the pathway. Most of the houses in the area were older, built in the late fifties or early sixties. The little bungalows all looked pretty similar. But with a view of the city skyline in the distance, and the Rocky Mountains beyond that, the lots along Twenty-Sixth Street were only fifteen minutes from downtown. Professionals were beginning to buy the little post-war houses, razing them to the ground and replacing them with designer mini-mansions. And why not? As the city council forced people to build up instead of out, people had to find a way to build their dream homes within the city limits.

"Look at that one!" Christina pointed to one of the big houses fronted with lots of tinted glass. She whistled and shook her head. "I can't believe anyone would spend the money to build something like that in the middle of the hood."

"I told you, it is not a hood."

Christina rolled her eyes.

Stella was enjoying herself, sniffing at the grass and weeds beside the pathway, wandering out as far as Margie would let her.

"It's an off-leash area," Christina told her, watching another dog playing chase with a ball. "You should let her run."

"Maybe when I know the area better. Right now… I'm not sure how responsible other people are with their dogs. You wouldn't want her to get hurt because someone else lets their dog off-leash when they shouldn't."

"Nothing would happen."

"That's what everyone always thinks. But some people are not responsible, and animals can turn in an instant, do something completely out of character because they felt threatened or excited by something."

They walked for a while in silence. There was a little viewing platform up ahead—a sort of a look-out point. Margie decided to check it out.

They stood looking down at Deerfoot and the Bow River and out at the city skyline glowing orange from the setting sun and, in the distance, the shadowy mountains.

"Isn't it gorgeous?" a man said. "No two sunsets are alike. I've heard that Calgary has some of the best in the world. I'm no world traveler, so I don't have much to compare it to, but this…" he gazed out at the city. "I never get tired of it."

Margie nodded. She studied his profile as he looked at the sunset. He wasn't wearing a mask. Mid-thirties or early forties. Good looking. Friendly and outgoing, apparently. A guy who probably would have shaken her hand before the pandemic. At his side was a large dog—a mutt like Stella, not something that Margie could classify.

"It is beautiful," she agreed. She looked at her watch. She should be heading back to Fish Creek Park to help canvass for witnesses and identify the faces caught on the tape.

"Oscar," the man said. "And this is Milo." He indicated the dog.

"I'm Margie. And this is my daughter, Christina, and Stella."

"You're not old enough to have a teenage daughter," Oscar challenged in a teasing tone.

"Well, that's a nice compliment. But believe me, I'm old enough and I feel it!"

Christina rolled her eyes as if she were being disparaged. "She was really young when she had me." In an *it's not my fault* tone.

"I don't remember seeing either of you here before. Do you live around here?"

"Just moved into the neighborhood," Margie agreed, making a motion back the way they had come. "Christina's been complaining about it, but I really like this." She looked out at the sky and the river. "And Fish Creek Park. I was just there this morning, and it's beautiful. Amazing to have such a big park right in the middle of the city."

"We're lucky to have these green spaces," Oscar agreed. He turned and pointed behind them, across Twenty-Sixth Street. "I'm just over there. If you cross here, there is a little park. There's a pond, a little waterpark for the kids, and volleyball courts with sand. A little gem hardly anybody knows about."

"Can we go over there?" Christina asked, moving away from them toward the crosswalk.

"I need to get home," Margie told her apologetically. "We can check it out tomorrow. But I have some work I need to do tonight."

Christina gave a heavy sigh. Life was hard for the kids of cops and working mothers.

CHAPTER SEVEN

Fish Creek Park had a different feeling as darkness started to fall and closing time approached. It was quiet. Voices carried, so people whispered or spoke in lowered tones as they walked. It was a slower pace, and the tang of wood smoke hung in the air from the campfires of earlier in the day.

Margie watched the shadows, thinking, drinking in the atmosphere. The weather conditions were almost the same as they had been the night Robinson was killed. She arrived at the same time as he had. She looked for the faces she had seen on the video surveillance, which she had carefully studied before arriving.

How easy would it have been for Robinson to be followed there by someone who intended to do him harm? He had left the pathway. She didn't know if he had still been visible from the path before he was killed. Maybe they should try a scene reconstruction just to test it out. Had his attacker gone there with the sole purpose of killing him? Had it been a drug deal or blackmail gone wrong? A quarrel between friends or lovers?

It wasn't robbery, that was about all Margie knew for sure. That, and it didn't look like a crime of passion.

She stopped a couple walking toward her, keeping the

prescribed two meters away since they were not wearing masks. "Excuse me. You were here two nights ago?"

They looked at each other, nodding automatically but then not sure if they should talk to her.

"I'm a homicide detective," Margie explained, pulling out her ID and showing it to them. "There was someone killed here, did you hear about it?"

"Yeah, we did." The woman, blond, a little shorter than Margie, nodded again. "I couldn't believe it. That happened in our park, where we walk, around the time that we were here." She said it with a tone of disbelief, as if it couldn't possibly be true.

Margie murmured confirmation at this.

"We didn't see anything suspicious." The woman looked at the man, getting a nod from him. "It was a night just like any other. Nothing… There wasn't anything that alarmed us."

"Anything out of the ordinary that night?" Margie asked. "Sounds, smells? Someone you don't normally see walking around here? Someone who seemed out of place or lost? Sick or afraid?"

The man put his arm around the woman and tightened his grip, pulling her to him protectively. "No," his voice was strong, slightly challenging. "Don't you have any leads? How could something like this happen here? I assumed that… it was drugs. A gang. Something where they knew each other. You always hear that in police reports. 'The victim was known to the killer.' They knew each other, right?"

"We are still very early in the investigation. We're hoping that you can help us with some background. Identify the people who normally walk around this time, help us to narrow the scope."

"Like what?" the woman asked. "What do you need us to do?"

"First of all, if I could get your information. Name, address, phone number, in case I need to contact you with further questions later."

They were a little reluctant. People were brought up not to share their personal information with strangers. They grew up watching cop shows on TV where people were suspects or were framed by the police. It was scary for them to be part of an investigation.

But also exciting. She could see their excitement at the novelty of being part of the investigation. A homicide investigation. Something most people had only ever seen on TV or read about in books.

Margie took down their information. Elise and Roger Erickson. Married ten years and still walking hand in hand every night in the park.

"I have some pictures on my tablet. I wonder if you could look at them, tell me who are regulars. What you know about them."

"Sure." This was the good part. The part where they could help her to break the case. They looked intently at the tablet as Margie moved a bit closer and brought up the first of the pictures. "Oh, that's Bob," Elise said confidently. "He doesn't like bicycles."

"Bicycles?" Margie repeated, not understanding.

"Bob is the dog," Roger laughed. "I think the detective wants the name of Bob's owner."

Margie chuckled. "Yes. That would be helpful."

"I don't know his owner's name… I just know Bob's name, because I hear him calling him, especially when Bob wants to chase after a bike."

Margie wrote down the information she had. "They walk here often?"

"Most nights. Most of the people who walk at this time of night are regulars. Day-trippers come during the day. Family reunions and parties in the late afternoon and evening. The people who walk late at night or early in the morning, they're all pretty regular."

Margie swiped to the next person on the tablet. Elise and Roger studied it.

"I've seen him," Roger said, "but I don't know anything about him."

"You said you thought maybe it was something to do with

drugs or gangs," Margie said. "Is that because you've seen drugs or gang activity in the park? Graffiti? People congregating? Something that makes you think that is going on?"

"No, I've never seen anything," Roger admitted. "I'm sure it goes on… it goes on everywhere, doesn't it? But I've never seen any drug deals going down or gangs. Or anything that I thought was. I just hoped… it isn't some crazy person, attacking at random…"

"I don't think that was the case here," Margie assured him. Very few homicides were random attacks. Maybe a robbery, someone with jewelry or a coat that made them look like they had a lot of money, but not random murders. "And if it is a serial killer, nobody has identified any pattern. Nothing that they had seen across a number of homicides."

They looked slightly reassured at this. Though Margie was kicking herself for using the words serial killer. That was only going to make them more worried, and they might use it when talking to other people, spreading the rumor that it was, in fact, a serial killer, when there was absolutely nothing to indicate that it was.

"If you could look at a few more people here…" She showed them the tablet again, swiping through the various people, most of whom they recognized. But they didn't have names to attach to a lot of them. At any rate, if they were frequent walkers in the park at that time of day, Margie would talk to them sooner or later.

She displayed the picture of the hooded figure. Elise shuddered. "Black hoodies always make me think of… Darth Vader or the Sith. Creepy, you know?"

"Do you recognize this person? We didn't get a very good picture of the face." Really, they hadn't captured anything of the face, just the hood and the shadows beneath it, as the hooded figure walked with head bowed past the camera. Margie didn't like it either. Not because it reminded her of the Sith, just because she didn't like anyone who appeared to have a reason to hide his face.

Who needed to hide his face in a park? Especially at night, when the shadows were already falling?

Maybe someone with a disfigurement. Otherwise, Margie couldn't think of a good reason, other than to avoid cameras and hide his identity.

"I've... I'm sure I've probably seen them here," Elise said slowly. "Not a lot, but a few times over the last week or two? Not every day. Or maybe he comes other times of the day, and not at the same time every night."

"Man or woman?" The figure was slim and could be either.

"A boy," Elise offered. "Not an adult. Maybe, sixteen? Umm... black. Not just brown, but very dark skin. I don't know..." She looked at her husband. "Maybe that's what made you think of drugs or gangs? Young Black man in a hoodie... if you watch much TV, it's sort of a trope." She shrugged, embarrassed. "I'm not racist; I'm not saying every kid in a hoodie is a drug dealer."

"I don't think it was anything like that," Roger protested, raising his hands in a 'stop' or 'surrender' motion. "I just wondered about drugs or gangs because it seems like that's where a lot of the violence stems from. Not because I saw him." He jerked his chin toward the hooded figure on the tablet and scratched the back of his neck. "I'm not judging anyone."

"We'll follow up on every possible lead. So you don't know his name or what area he lives in? Was he ever here with someone else?"

"No." They both looked at each other for confirmation and shook their heads at the same time. "No, we never talked to him or left at the same time. And he's always alone."

Margie thanked them for their time when they were finished looking through all of the pictures. Even though she didn't have many names or details, she felt like she was making progress. Lots of the people whose pictures she had clipped would be walking through the park just then. Margie would find them and talk with them, slowly gathering identities and alibis and sorting out who she felt was suspicious and warranted further attention.

THE CANVASS SLOWED TO A TRICKLE, and then a stop. There was no one left on the pathways but the detectives themselves. They converged and began comparing notes as they walked back to their vehicles.

"Some nice folks out here," Jones commented. She seemed to be walking a little gingerly, and Margie watched her, trying to figure out whether she had turned her ankle or had blisters or something else. "Reminds me that I don't take advantage of the parks around here often enough. We complain about being stuck in the city, but there is all of this… wilderness right here in the middle of it."

"I was really excited about that when I started to look at Calgary," Margie agreed. "I like walking and hiking and biking, and I'm looking forward to being able to check out the different parks and pathways in Calgary. There are so many places to go."

"I *think* that I like walking until I'm actually on my feet for a few hours like this," Jones said. "And then my feet start to hurt, and I start to chafe, and then I realize that I really *don't* like it very much at all."

Margie laughed. "Don't go right from being sedentary to walking for a few hours. Do it gradually; your body will adjust."

Jones smoothed her hands over her broad hips and grimaced. "Yeah. One step at a time," she agreed.

"Who on your list do you want to follow up on?" Siever asked. "We still have lots more video that we can check. Spy on people the whole time they were at the park."

"There are a few I'd like to look into further," Margie admitted. "Of course, everyone who wasn't here tonight, but the man with the pit bull and the young man in the hoodie in particular."

"Don't tell me you have a thing about pitties," Siever challenged, "sweetest disposition you ever saw…"

"I didn't say anything in particular about the dog or the breed," Margie said. "Everybody has their own opinion about that.

I just mean I'd like to take a closer look at the owner. He rubbed me the wrong way. I want to explore the possibility that he might have gotten into an argument with Mr. Robinson."

"Could have," Siever agreed, nodding. "He didn't look like the most laid-back guy."

"But why would he come to walk in the park if he was that irritable?" Jones asked. "If you're spoiling to pick a fight, why go to a park? Why not a bar or somewhere else he could have blown off some steam?"

Siever shrugged. "Maybe he didn't want to get in a fight. Maybe he was trying to work off whatever stress he was feeling so that he could relax and *not* get in a fight."

"I suppose."

"Walking somewhere like this is peaceful. Get in touch with your serenity. Put all of the stress of the day behind you."

Jones nodded. "Okay. Maybe."

"I'd still like to look into him further," Margie repeated.

"Of course. We'll see if we can spot him on some of the other video, follow him back, see where he came from and went to and the times. Everyone we have pictures of was here at roughly the right time. We can't eliminate anyone just by having one conversation with them."

No, there would be a lot of footwork and further discussions to eliminate people from their lists. Like all police work, it was long hours of tedium, followed by moments of intense action or terror. It would take a long time to look through the videos to find everybody and identify their movements, and then try to find any connections with Robinson other than that they had just happened to be in the park at the same time.

Could anyone put them together? Did they walk together? Have a business? Were they friends? Lovers? Enemies? In a club? Share a vice? Lots of questions to be asked.

CHAPTER EIGHT

Margie was watching videos again the next morning. The camera locations had been plotted on a map, which was helpful, so that she could try to find people again after they walked off of one camera. Follow the trail until it came to another camera, and then watch for them to appear there. If they didn't appear, then look at some of the places it might branch off to a different location. Or had they gone off trail completely, and wouldn't reconnect with it again for several hours?

It was tedious work, but she created a profile for each person who had been at the park at the same time as Robinson, included their picture and, if they had it, the person's name and any other details they had. She ignored, for the time being, anyone who they had gathered identification and contact details from. It was more important to track down the people who hadn't come forward or returned to the park as usual. Those were the people who were more likely to have had something to do with Robinson's death. Someone who hoped that by staying away for a few days, or permanently, that he would be able to distance himself from the investigation and maybe stay below the radar.

She had identified the man with the pit bull by following his images on the videos back to the parking lot and getting the license plate from his car. That was a lucky break. With the name on the car's registration, she was able to look up his driver's license and confirm that it matched the face on the video. They would gather his contact information and pay him a visit.

Margie was having a more difficult time with the boy in the hoodie. She peered at the screen, trying to track him as he moved from one camera to another like a ghost. His dark outfit blended in with the shadows, and he drifted rather than walked along the pathway.

"Any luck?" Cruz's voice at Margie's shoulder made her startle. She looked around at him, blowing out her breath.

"You mind not sneaking up on me? Next time I might go for my gun."

He raised his brows, knowing full well that her gun was locked away while she was at her desk, the same as everyone else's. It wasn't really much of a threat. Margie shook her head.

"Working on it. Fitting together one piece of the puzzle at a time."

"You think this kid had anything to do with it?" He indicated the screen.

Margie took a deep breath, studying the young man on the monitor as if it were the first time she had seen him. "I really don't. What reason would he have to be involved with someone like Robinson? An adult. A welder. Not the kind of person he would have hung out with. No sign that it was robbery or drugs. A random attack? It's possible, but I don't think so."

"But you're still going to track him down."

"Of course."

Cruz nodded. "Have fun."

"You're welcome to take a video any time you like. I don't mean to hog all of the fun stuff."

He grinned. "No, no, you're the new one here. You should have the opportunity for as much investigative work as you want." He straightened his shirt, a bold pink color that apparently was no threat to his manhood.

"There's plenty to go around. I promise."

"I've got other files to work. This is your first, so you can put your full attention into it," he told her sagely, smiling but no longer joking. "See what you can dig up."

Margie went back to work trying to track the hoodie boy.

AFTER TRACKING the boy's walk through the park, they needed more. He had not taken a vehicle into the park, but had walked in. Video from traffic cams, security surveillance, private house-holders, whatever they could get. That meant Margie and the other detectives getting out on the street to spot all of the cameras they could and to track him half a block at a time as they back-tracked his arrival and then requesting the video from the owner. The footage taken in the daylight hours when he had arrived was much easier to see than the nighttime footage after he had left.

More than once, she asked herself why she was doing it. They had a lot of people they hadn't yet eliminated. She was working on them too. But the boy who had arrived on foot with his face hidden was suspicious. He wasn't there with friends, wasn't there to work out, and appeared to be intentionally hiding his face from the cameras or the other patrons of the park. What was he doing there?

"Got him!" Jones said, banging her keyboard and sitting back in her chair.

Margie looked over at her. "Got him?"

"The boy. I have him coming out of a house." Jones smiled like the cat who caught the canary, then gave Margie the address.

"Shall we go check it out?" Margie suggested.

"You want me to come?"

"You're the one who got the address. I think you should. Unless you don't want to…"

"Oh, I want to!" Jones pushed back from her desk. "Let's do it."

≈

MARGIE LOOKED at her watch as they arrived at the house. It was afternoon and, if they were lucky, the boy would be home from school. Back in Forest Lawn, Christina would be getting on the bus. It would be half an hour before she was home. Hopefully, this boy's school was within walking distance of his home. From what she had seen, though, the newer areas were farther away from schools. Or the boy might be one of the kids accessing online schooling during the pandemic and was therefore home during the day.

She raised her hand and knocked loudly on the door. A good, authoritative knock. The kind that made people take notice instead of deciding that since they weren't expecting any friends or deliveries, they would just ignore the door and hope that the salesperson or missionaries went on to the next house.

In about half a minute, she could hear footsteps from within, and a man came to the door. Tall and skinny. Taller than the boy on the footage. Not a teenager. His skin was very dark, just as the boy's had been reported to be. Margie decided to go with it.

"We're here looking for your son, is he home?" she asked.

He looked confused. "My son?" Then he gave his head a little shake. "Oh. Yes. Abdul."

Abdul. Margie made a mental note of it. The man had a thick accent. She wasn't sure where he was from. "Is Abdul home?"

"No. He's not back from school yet." The man looked to the side as if studying something. "He is not working today, so he will probably be home in... about half an hour?"

"Could we come in, please? We should probably talk to you before he gets home."

He looked down, frowning. Searching for a way to tell them no. He didn't want the police in his house. He didn't seem curious to know what they wanted with his son; he just wanted them to leave. Wanted a way to tell them to go. But after standing there silently for a few uncomfortable seconds, he stepped back and opened the door farther to allow them entrance.

Margie and Jones stepped in. The living room was plainly furnished. An older couch and some easy chairs. A TV on a stand. A colorful tapestry hung on the wall, and another draped over the couch, but there were no paintings or prints. The man made a motion toward the couch. Margie looked around once more. She didn't hear anyone else in the house. She didn't see any sign of drugs, weapons, or anything else that raised red flags. She met Jones's eyes to make sure she felt the same way and didn't see any concerns there. They sat down.

"What's your last name?" Margie asked, pulling out her notepad and writing *Abdul* on a fresh page.

"Paul."

"Paul is your last name?" she checked. "Not your first?"

He nodded. "Sadiq is my first name."

"Sadiq Paul?" Margie spelled it out as she wrote it, and he nodded his agreement. But the way that his eyes stayed on her face, she wondered if she had spelled too fast and he was still trying to catch up with her. English was not his first language.

"And is that Abdul's last name too?"

"No." He shook his head. "Abdul's last name is James."

"Got it." Margie wrote it down. "Did he take his mother's name, then?"

The man gave a shrug that Margie wasn't sure how to interpret. Yes, it was his mother's name? Or there was some other reason he had a different last name?

"Can you tell me where Abdul was three nights ago?"

"Three nights. He was here. He is always here. This is his home."

"Before bed," Margie clarified. "Say, between school and bedtime. He wasn't here the whole time."

"No. It takes time for him to get home from school. And some nights he works." This time, Margie saw the schedule on the whiteboard he had been looking at previously. Her eyes went to the night of Robinson's death. No shift was noted for Abdul. He should have been home.

"Where would he have gone if he wasn't working? He doesn't come straight home."

"He comes home for supper. Always home for supper, if he's not working."

"And then he goes out again after that?"

"Sometimes," Sadiq agreed.

"Where does he go when he goes out again in the evening and he doesn't have work?"

"I don't ask him. Sometimes, just walking around the neighborhood. Maybe to a friend's house. Sometimes to the park."

"Fish Creek Park?"

"Yes." His head turned in the direction of the park. "It's a good place to walk. To… reconnect with yourself after a long day."

"Do you go with him?"

"No." Sadiq shook his head firmly. "I don't get in his way. He wants to walk alone."

"I see. So you don't supervise him and you don't ask him to account for where he has been."

Sadiq shook his head and didn't offer any explanation. Maybe that was normal in the culture and background he came from. Many Indigenous parents let their children explore on their own and take care of themselves much more than their white counterparts. It taught interdependence with the land. Learning to live in harmony with others and the environment. Perhaps it was the same where this man came from. Margie wrote a few notes.

"Maybe while we are waiting for Abdul to get home, we could see his room."

Sadiq didn't move. Margie waited. He didn't offer any objection or give permission. Margie cut her eyes toward Jones. Did his silence indicate consent? Could they go ahead and look for Abdul's room, and if Sadiq didn't object, take that as his consent to a search? Or at least to a look around at what was in plain sight? Jones grimaced, not offering her opinion one way or the other.

Margie didn't feel right about it. There was, if nothing more, a communication gap. She didn't want to get herself in trouble for an illegal search and risk having important evidence thrown out.

"Could we look at Abdul's room?" she asked more plainly.

Sadiq looked at her. At first, she thought he was going to shrug, still not understanding exactly what she wanted from him, and that shrug might be able to be taken as consent. But he didn't shrug. He shook his head.

"We can't see Abdul's room?" Jones pressed. "What are you trying to hide?"

"It is not my place to give permission for you to see his room. That is his space. He can decide when he is here."

So they waited. Margie thought of more questions about Abdul and asked them here and there, but was no closer to understanding the situation of the father and son than she had been when he answered the door. Was there a wife and mother around? There didn't seem to be. Had Abdul always been with Sadiq, or was it a recent development?

"Where did you come here from?"

Sadiq considered, not answering immediately. Was he worried they would judge him? Eventually, he decided to answer.

"We are from the Sudan."

And then Abdul was there. Margie hadn't even heard the door open and close, and Abdul was standing just a few feet away from her, the black hood pulled up over his head just as it had been when he had walked through the park. Maybe the permanent state of affairs. He had on a black bandana mask, pulled up high, so that when she looked into the depths of the hood, all she could see was the glitter of his eyes.

"Abdul." Margie got to her feet, and the boy took a couple of quick steps back. "No, it's okay. We just wanted to talk to you."

He looked at his father and then back at Margie again. He pulled the bandana down to his neck, revealing fine features, midway between child and adult. Vulnerable and not yet the man's face he would grow into. But no longer quite a child, either.

"You are po-lice?" he asked in a soft voice, still high in pitch.

Margie tried to make her nod as reassuring as possible. She didn't want him running away. Kids tended to be anxious around the police even if they hadn't done anything against the law. It was part of the mindset at that age.

"Yes, we are both police detectives." She was glad she had brought Jones instead of one of the male detectives. They would not be as threatening to Abdul. "My name is Detective Patenaude and this is Detective Jones. We wanted to ask you about your walk in the park the other day."

He studied Jones and then looked back at Margie. "What day? I walk in park many days."

"Three days ago. In the evening. You were there almost until closing time. Ten o'clock."

He nodded.

"Do you remember?"

A small shrug. A look around at his surroundings for confirmation that he was still safe in his own home. He sat down on the arm of Sadiq's chair. He pulled back his hood, revealing short-cropped curly black hair. There were scars on his face. Not abuse, she didn't think. Maybe a childhood accident. "I remember."

"I want you to think about whether you saw or heard anything unusual that night. Maybe… shouting or an argument? Somebody that you hadn't seen at the park before or who scared you. Anything… that we might be interested in."

"What is this about?" Sadiq asked, his pronunciation overly precise. She was surprised that he hadn't asked before. The police showed up at the door asking for his son and he didn't even ask why?

Margie didn't answer him, but pulled out her tablet and selected a picture of Robinson. Not a picture of his body, but the one from his driver's license. She held it up for Abdul. "Did you see this man?"

Abdul looked at it. He reached out tentatively and Margie handed it to him. He brought it close to his eyes, studying it. Was he supposed to wear glasses? When had he last had his vision checked? Maybe never. They were immigrants; maybe they hadn't availed themselves of the province's health services.

After a while, Abdul handed the tablet back. "I have seen this man before. Other days."

"But not three days ago?"

His shoulders lifted and fell. "I do not remember. That day?" He shook his head. "Maybe and maybe not. I know the face."

"Do you know his name? Have you ever stopped to talk to him?"

Abdul's eyes skittered away. "No," he said in a low voice. "Why would I talk to him? What reason would he have to talk to me?"

"The other day, when I was out in a park near my house walking my dog, another man who was walking his dog commented to me what a beautiful sunset it was. We talked for a few minutes, just about the sky and the park and what it was like to live in the neighborhood." She let him think about that for a minute. "Maybe you had a conversation like that with Mr. Robinson."

"No. He never stops me to tell me it is a beautiful day."

Put like that, it did seem a little silly. A man and a woman of similar age might stop to chat, but a white man and a Black teenager?

"You have a dog?" Abdul asked, showing interest in something for the first time.

"Yes." Margie smiled at him. "Would you like to see a picture?" She pulled out her phone, selected the photos app, and found one of Stella, mouth wide in a panting doggie grin as if she had been posing for the picture. She handed it over to Abdul.

A little smile formed on his face. He touched the screen lightly as if he could introduce himself to Stella that way or reach through the screen to pet her. He swiped, looking at other photos. "Is this your daughter?"

"Yes. She must be about your age. Are you fifteen? Sixteen?"

"Fourteen," he corrected. "I am very tall."

"Yes. You are tall for fourteen. Christina is fifteen." Margie reached over and took the phone out of his hands. He didn't need to be looking through the rest of her pictures. It wasn't like she had taken pictures of anything private or inappropriate. Or had crime scene photos on it. She just didn't think he needed to be looking at pictures of her life. They were there to talk about him. His life, and how Jerry Robinson's life had ended.

Abdul's hands fell to his lap and stayed there. He didn't fidget. He just watched them. Margie couldn't imagine this frail-looking fourteen-year-old having a fight with Robinson. Physical or verbal. He was shy and uncertain. He wouldn't have a reason to approach Robinson. He said they had never talked.

He didn't appear to have any concern about talking about being in the park that night. He probably hadn't even heard that there had been a death. If Sadiq had read about it in the paper or online, maybe he had hidden it from Abdul, deciding that he didn't need to be upset by it. But Margie suspected Sadiq didn't even read the news. It wouldn't be relaxing for him to read it in a language other than his native tongue.

"The reason that we're asking questions is that man I showed you died that night."

Abdul's eyes got wide. "He died?"

"Yes. He was killed."

Abdul looked at her for a moment as if trying to translate what she had said. Maybe he was. Perhaps the shades of meaning between *he died* and *he was killed* hadn't occurred to him before and needed some thought.

"Somebody killed him?" Abdul asked. "He not just…" He clutched at his chest, miming before he found the words. "Heart attack?"

"That's right. Somebody killed him."

"Was he shot?" Sadiq asked.

Margie shook her head. She looked at Abdul, waiting for his reaction. Watching for any recollection in his eyes of something that had happened that day. He looked at his father, considering his words, and then back at Margie again.

"That is very bad," he said. "But I do not know who hurt him."

He looked directly at her with his wide, brown eyes, and Margie did not sense any deception.

CHAPTER NINE

Back at the office, Margie and Jones huddled with the other detectives who were there.

"I don't think it's the kid," Margie said. She looked at Jones. "Do you concur?"

Jones nodded slowly. "He didn't strike me as being guilty or evasive. Shy, yes, and feeling his way through things. He's clearly a recent immigrant, still learning the language and the culture."

"Is he in a gang?" Cruz asked. "That black hoodie has me wondering. Just what is he trying to hide? You know that one of the reasons bangers wear loose clothing is to hide weapons. And the hoods hide people's faces, make it harder for them to identify. You're sure that's not what's going on here? Sometimes immigrants band together for safety."

"He's probably cold," Jones said. "If he came here from an African country, then he's probably freezing, even when we would consider it warm. And at nightfall, it gets quite chilly. Under ten. I don't like to go out without a hoodie at that time."

"He was wearing a face mask," Margie said. "And that could indicate that he's trying to hide his identity... or just that he's following the rules for when he is at school or on the bus. He did take it off when we introduced ourselves."

"No suspicious behavior?" Cruz challenged. "You know that these kids can be pretty glib. They've always got a story, a disarming smile. They don't necessarily act like the hoods you see on TV."

"Not my first rodeo," Margie sighed. "I've dealt with plenty of gang kids in Manitoba. I don't think they're that different here. I didn't see any sign that he was affiliated with a gang or might have any sort of freelance drug business."

"And the father? It could be the parents. They need something to stay solvent. They get the kids to traffic, but it's really the parents who are the problem."

"No. Nothing that gave me any clue that there were illegal drugs. Or fencing or any other kind of illegal or quasi-legal side hustle I can think of. They appear to be new immigrants, just trying to start a new life for themselves."

Cruz nodded slowly. "Okay. So you're pretty sure that the kid didn't have anything to do with it. Too bad, I liked the dark hooded suspect. So it's back to the drawing board. We still have a few people we haven't been able to identify. A couple of cyclists. They would be able to get away from the scene more quickly. They could have gotten there from another part of the city, farther afield. Who else is on your suspicious persons list?"

"We have more people still on it than have been eliminated," Margie admitted. "I'll spend some time tomorrow trying to establish any connections between them and Robinson."

"Sounds like a plan," Mac contributed. He had remained silent up until that point. "I think we have as much from the video as we are going to get right now. We might have to review some footage down the line, but we only have a limited number of suspects. Like one of those closed-room mysteries. It shouldn't be too hard to figure out who had a grudge against Robinson."

"In those mysteries, everyone has a grudge," Margie said. "There is always a secret lover, an illegitimate baby, an angry business partner, a spy…"

"Then we'd better get to it," MacDonald said. "Or Inspector

Poirot will beat us to it." He looked at his watch. "Tomorrow. Get a good sleep tonight and start fresh."

❦

"CAN we check out that park today?" Christina asked as Margie slid on her shoes to take Stella out for a walk. "You know, the one with the pond," Christina reminded her, when Margie just looked at her blankly, trying to figure out if Christina meant she wanted to go to Fish Creek Park. "The one that Grouch guy told us about?"

"Oh!" Recollection started to return. "You mean… Oscar. The one with the dog, Milo."

"Yeah, Oscar." Christina giggled at her mistake. "That's what I meant. He said there was a park over there, by the viewing platform. Across the street."

"Okay. Sure. We can check it out. We don't have a lot of time before it gets dark, though, so we won't be able to stay and explore for long."

"Yay!" Christina slid on a pair of sandals. "I didn't know there was a waterpark so close. That will be nice when it's hot out."

Margie nodded her agreement and snapped the leash onto Stella's collar. "Okay, girl! Let's go! Let's go walkie."

Margie was cautiously optimistic. Christina seemed to be in better spirits today. Margie didn't ask whether Christina had had a good day at school or whether she had made some new friends. Questions like that just seemed to irritate the girl and remind her that she was supposed to be sullen and angry about the move. So they just walked, laughed at Stella's antics, looked at the houses and the other people enjoying the pathway, and talked about other things. When Christina was ready to talk about her classes or her friends, she would.

At the viewing platform, they turned and used the crosswalk across to the other side, to what a chiseled-rock sign declared to be Valleyview Park. They walked to the top of a little hill, looked down at the pond, at the playground enclosed in a fence, and the field and sand courts beyond it.

"I was expecting… like, waterslides." Christina's disappointment was evident. "Not just a little kids' splash park."

"I'm sorry. I had no idea what it would be like. I guess this is what passes for a waterpark in the hood," Margie said, hoping to raise a smile.

Christina rolled her eyes. "Well… let's at least walk around the pond."

There were soccer goals in the open field next to the pond. "This would be a good place to throw the ball around," Margie observed. "I don't want to do it over by the ditch, for fear Stella would run right off of the edge and hurt herself. But lots of space over there and away from any traffic."

"It would be good for balls or Frisbee," Christina agreed. She scratched Stella's ears. "Next time, we'll play here for a while."

They nodded and smiled at other people walking around the pond or sitting on the benches nearby. There were walkers, kids on tiny bikes, and an old man on an electric scooter who smiled and talked to everyone who approached him. Margie was enjoying the friendliness of Calgary. She was glad that she had taken the job there.

As they walked back home, Margie talked about Abdul. Not by name, of course, and not in connection with the Fish Creek Park murder. Just casually as a boy that she had talked to that day. She folded her arms, cuddling her sweatshirt closer, remembering how Jones had suggested Abdul was probably always cold after coming from a warmer climate.

"It would be a lot worse coming from Sudan than from Winnipeg," Christina admitted, staring off at the city skyline as they walked the path along Twenty-sixth Street toward home. "I mean… I'm looking forward to the Chinooks. To the winters being a lot easier than in Manitoba. And it would be like… a totally different culture. I might not have any friends here yet, but at least I know how things work, and what to expect at school and all that. Could he even read when he came here?"

"I have no idea. They didn't say he was in any special program at school, but I didn't ask, either. It was clear that English was not his native language."

"Ugh. I can't imagine having to learn a whole new language. Thanks for not moving to… Germany or something like that. Or Norway. It's cold there, right?"

"Yes, it gets cold there."

"I'm glad we stayed in Canada. Having to deal with all of that other stuff… that would be a lot harder."

Margie was glad to see that Christina could see she hadn't had it as bad as some people did. She really was a good girl. It was just hard to stay focused on everything she had to be grateful for.

They walked along in silence for a few minutes.

"Hey, there's the guy again. Milo and…?"

"Oscar." Margie waved as they got closer. "Hi, Oscar."

The dogs sniffed each other and pranced around. "Enjoying the weather?" Oscar asked.

"May as well enjoy it while we can. It's not going to last forever." Even though Margie was a little chilly in just a hoodie, she knew better than to complain about it. A few more weeks, and there would be snow on the ground and much lower temperatures.

"Yeah, you're right," Oscar agreed. "There's no keeping winter from coming."

And would business slow down with the cold weather? Margie knew that it wouldn't. Cold weather didn't stop people from killing each other. It might help with hiding bodies until the next melt, but people who were forced to live inside at close quarters tended to get on each other's nerves. And when they got into the pre-Christmas season, then not only would the murder rate go up due to the stress and other crazy stuff that happened around the holidays, but so would the suicide rate. And suicides were investigated by the homicide department. It would be a busy time—

Christmas, New Year, and then the long, cold, interminable nights of February. Margie couldn't suppress a little shudder. Christina looked at her but didn't say anything.

They talked for a few more minutes with Oscar and Milo before returning home.

CHAPTER TEN

*M*argie would be glad to get home after a long day in front of her computer. Her time had been broken up with various phone calls and emails to follow up on possible leads, ask some more questions, and to establish either alibis for Robinson's murder or connections with him. Computer databases, web searches, talking to neighbors, Robinson's coworkers, and anyone who might be identified as friends. He seemed to have lived a pretty solitary life, and finding even tentative connections was a slog.

By the end of it, she felt like her brain had been wrung out. Her nerves and her emotions were raw. She needed to get home to her daughter and Stella, to spend some time outside in the fresh air and to move around and get some exercise. She had known that there would be a lot of desk work associated with homicide work. That just went with the territory.

As she put her office tools away into the drawers, she tried to mentally do the same with the day's stresses and worries. A ceremonial laying aside of her work life. She would try not to take any burdens home with her, but to go home lighter and happier.

She plugged her phone into the car stereo and tapped a few times to bring up her de-stress playlist. A broadly-ranging combination of Métis fiddlers, classic rock, and rap to help exorcise the demons of the office.

The rest of the week, she had managed to get home before Christina, but this time the front door was unlocked and she knew she had worked too late. She glanced at her watch before entering.

"Hi, honey. Sorry to be so long today. How was school?"

There was no answer. Christina wasn't in the living room or kitchen. Margie went down the hallway to peek in Christina's door to see if she was doing her homework with her headphones on.

Christina wasn't in her bedroom. Margie's stomach clenched. She looked back toward the front door. She was sure she had locked it that morning. Christina was home. She wouldn't still be at school or on the bus that late. Christina had arrived home and had unlocked the door.

Margie continued down the hall to the bathroom, but the door stood ajar and it was clear that Christina was not there either.

"Christina? Are you here?"

Margie exited the hall into the kitchen.

"Christina?"

She heard a volley of barks from Stella in the backyard and blew out her breath in a sigh of relief. Of course, Christina had just taken Stella outside.

Then there was a shrill shriek of fear or alarm. Margie ran to the back door and out into the yard.

"Christina? What is it?"

Christina ran to her, colliding on the step and putting her arms around Margie.

"What is it? What's wrong?"

Christina made a sobbing, choking noise. Margie looked for Stella, worried that she had run out of the yard and been hit by a car in the back lane. But Stella was standing in the middle of the back yard, looking happy and relaxed, not understanding why her young master was upset. Margie didn't get it either. She pushed Christina away from her to look at her face.

"Christina! Talk to me!"

Christina shook her head. "No, it's okay," she said, even though her expression was still distressed. She seemed unable to say anything else to explain herself.

Margie hugged her, pulling her close again and holding Christina firmly to try to convey strength and calm to her. Christina sniffled a few times and then pulled back.

"It's fine. I'm okay. Everything is fine," she again reassured Margie.

"Okay. Take a deep breath and then tell me what happened."

"Come." Christina stepped back and gave Margie's arm a little tug to encourage her to follow. She walked across the yard toward Stella. Stella started to bound around excitedly, wanting to play or show off about something. Christina pointed to a clump of leaves on the grass.

Margie took a closer look and saw that it wasn't a clump of sod and dead brown grass, but the body of a dead squirrel.

"Oh." Margie sighed. "It's okay. I'll just get rid of it."

Christina made a face. "I thought it was just some twigs. I was going to pick up a stick to throw for Stella, and then I realized…" She gagged. "Ugh. I almost picked it up!"

And that had given her quite a start.

"Try not to keep visualizing it," Margie advised. "If you can distract yourself with other things, it won't be saved as such a vivid memory. The less you think about it, the faster it will fade."

Christina ran her hands over her face as if trying to wipe it away. "Will you…?" She made a motion toward the squirrel.

"I'll take care of it. Why don't you get started on some dinner? Just let me grab some paper towel first so that I won't be in your way."

They went back into the house. Margie called Stella in. She didn't want the dog to get in the way while she was trying to deal with the squirrel. Especially if Stella thought it was some new game for her and tried to take the squirrel back away from her.

"You stay in here," she told Stella sternly. "Go lie down. I'll get you a treat when I come back in."

"Mom?"

Margie looked at Christina.

"You don't think… Stella didn't kill it, did she?"

"No, I'm sure she didn't," Margie assured her. "She likes to chase squirrels, but she's never caught one. I don't think she'd have any idea what to do with it if she did."

"Yeah." Christina's face relaxed, her relief clear. "Yeah, you're right."

She turned to the cupboard to look for something to make for supper. Margie went back outside with her handful of paper towels. She approached the squirrel's corpse with trepidation.

Which was pretty funny, considering what she did for a living. Why should she be anxious about a dead squirrel? She, who dealt with dead people all day long? A dead squirrel wasn't even going to hold a candle to the horrors of murdered men, women, and children that she had seen and would yet see in the future.

She picked it up in the paper towel. She had planned to just throw it straight into the green bin without looking at it, but she heard Christina's question in her mind and had to make sure that Stella could not have killed it. If she had, they would have to make sure that she was not allowed outside on her own. She would always have to be supervised until they were sure that she wasn't a squirrel-killer.

The body was stiff. Not a fresh kill. Margie squinted at it, looking for bite marks. Looking for the injury that had killed it. There were many ways a squirrel could die. It could have eaten poisoned mouse bait. It could have been electrocuted running on one of the power lines. It could have been hit by a car, killed by a cat or another dog. How it got into her yard was another story. But an animal could have dragged it there. A person walking down the back lane could have picked it up and thrown it over the fence. Why, she didn't quite know, but it was possible. People were highly unpredictable.

There was dried blood on the torso. It looked like a clean edge, not a bite mark. Not any of the accidents that she had thought might befall an unwary squirrel. But there could be other things. Something sharp… on the ground… or a barbed -wire fence… maybe a tin can that the squirrel had crawled into, looking for nuts or something that had smelled good. What looked like a knife edge could have been a dozen other things. She wasn't a medical examiner. She wasn't performing a necropsy and trying to analyze who or what had killed the squirrel. She just wanted to make sure that it hadn't been Stella, and it hadn't been.

Margie walked briskly to the back gate and out into the alley to toss the body into the green bin. She made sure it was well-wrapped and then threw more paper towels down on top of it, so that she would never have to see it again.

Rest in peace, little squirrel.

Margie went back into the house to help Christina prepare supper.

CHAPTER ELEVEN

The next morning as they prepared for the day ahead, Christina asked, "Mom, could we go see Moushoom again? Maybe after school today?"

Margie considered her workload and schedule for the day and nodded. "I'll try to get home around the same time as you do, and we'll go over. The staff said he could eat what he wanted, so we could take him food this time."

"Burgers?" Christina suggested.

"If that's what you want, sure. I'm sure he would like that."

"Do you think he would like something else better? Could we make him something traditional? Something he hasn't had for a long time and that you can't buy in the restaurants?"

Margie blinked. "What a great idea. I'm sure he would just love that. I don't have a lot of time and energy after work, though, I don't think we can make anything too ambitious."

"Maybe we could just make bannock this time, but we could plan something else next time. When we have more time to shop and prepare."

"Perfect. Great idea. You don't need many ingredients for bannock, so I think I can manage that without a shopping trip. Somebody said it's harder to bake in Calgary because of the altitude, so it might not turn out quite the way we expect. We might have to try a few different times before we get it just right. It's just a matter of learning how to cook in a new environment."

"How does the altitude affect baking?"

"I'm not sure. I'll have to look it up. I know that water doesn't boil at the same temperature."

Christina looked at her like she was crazy. "Water always boils at the same temperature. One hundred degrees."

"One hundred degrees at sea level."

Christina shook her head, still not believing it. She wedged more books into her bag and looked across the room out to the street.

"There's the bus! I gotta run!"

Margie wasn't even sure if Christina heard her 'goodbye' as she belted out of the house. There was certainly not going to be any hug and kiss and sage motherly advice that morning. It would have to wait until their visit with Moushoom.

❧

SHE WAS glad after work that they were going to visit Moushoom. She needed something to help take her head out of her work, and her de-stress playlist had not done it. She and Christina put their heads together in the kitchen to make a batch of bannock, which had turned out fine despite Margie's misgivings. Maybe bannock was just one of those recipes that was impossible to screw up. They wrapped it up so it would still be warm from the stove when they got to Moushoom's apartment.

When they reached Moushoom's room, they again found him parked in front of the TV. Moushoom beamed at them and waved his hand at the TV. "You can shut that off. The nurses are always turning on the TV's to keep people quiet. And after trying to ignore it for a while… you kind of get dragged into it. But I don't want it on while my granddaughters are here to see me!"

Margie moved a TV table over Moushoom's knees and put

down her bundle. "Wait until you see what we brought for you. This was Christina's idea."

Christina ducked her head and looked shy, but also excited and proud. "We made it together."

"Bannock!" Moushoom exclaimed in delight. "I don't remember when the last time I had bannock was!" He immediately broke off a piece and popped it into his mouth. "This is the best thing you could have brought me. It takes me right back to my childhood; sitting in my mother's kitchen, eating the bannock hot from the stove. Even in hard times, there was still bannock to fill hungry tummies."

He closed his eyes, savoring it. He opened them again.

"Come on, come on. Bring chairs over. You come have some too. We'll have a proper little feast here. Like we were away at school, sneaking food after lights out."

Margie and Christina did as he instructed. Margie laid out the butter and jam that she had brought along. She thought about what it had been like for Moushoom, back in the days of residential school, when the white man was so intent on beating the Indian out of the children. Anything that reminded them of their own culture had been banned. The Indigenous languages, spiritual beliefs, clothing, food, and ceremonies. They cut off their hair like the Philistines in the Christian Bible, trying to take away Samson's strength.

"Eat, eat," Moushoom encouraged, bringing Margie back to the present. She smiled at him and broke a piece off, eating while smiling at him. The white man had failed. They had not been able to steal Moushoom's culture away from him. They had not been able to stamp out all of the Indigenous cultures, though they had tried their best.

They sat down, lowering their masks to eat. Margie hoped that they were far enough apart to prevent an infection. She didn't want Moushoom getting sick. Sharing food and the knife for the butter was not a good idea, but they had both sanitized their hands before taking the elevator up.

"It must have been awful for you, going away to school," Margie said.

Moushoom's smile dimmed. He closed his eyes for a moment against the unwelcome memories, then shook it off and looked at her with a confident smile. "We learned far more than the brothers ever intended to teach us. They thought that they could crush us. Could squash the Métis out of us. We were like prisoners of war. But we were warriors. They could not overcome us."

He nibbled at some more bannock.

"Not all of us," he admitted. "Many of my brothers and sisters never came home." He looked at Christina and shook his head. "You seem so young to me now, but you are as old as I was when I left that place, a full-grown man, expected to fend for myself. A fully-educated man, looking and acting like a white man. You wouldn't believe it if you saw pictures of me then. But I went back to my people, grew my hair out, put on my sash, and I never let my culture go. Even when I came west and settled here, I didn't pretend to be white. I am Métis. I will always be Métis."

Christina nodded. She lifted her chin a little. "I am too. I'm still going to school. I want to get my education, but not so that I can be like them."

"There is nothing wrong with being educated. As long as you don't let them write their stories on your heart."

"I won't."

"Good girl."

Margie let her eyes drift around the room as she buttered and ate small pieces of the bannock, making it last as long as she could. Like Abdul's house, it was starkly furnished. Moushoom had not been able to bring many of his possessions there. But there were still decorations intended to remind him of his heritage. And he wore as much traditional clothing as he could.

There were certain parallels between Moushoom and the immigrants. Even though they represented opposite ends of the spectrum, one preserving his old traditions and the immigrants trying to adapt to an entirely new culture, they were similar to each other, out-of-step with the mainstream. Outsiders.

At least Abdul did not have to experience what Moushoom had. He went to public school with other children of all different races and traditions, and there was no one telling him that he could not keep his own name, no one shaving his head or beating him if he spoke his own language or didn't answer a question the way that they wanted him to. There were still rules, but they were not brutal and were not designed to erase who he was.

"What are you thinking of?" Moushoom asked.

"A boy I interviewed recently. He is from the Sudan, in Africa. Very far away and very different from the children here. I was talking to Christina the other day about how hard it must be for him to adjust to a new language and culture. Like you did."

Moushoom nodded his understanding. His dark eyes shone with interest and intelligence. There had been stories before Margie had moved to Calgary, suggesting that he was growing senile, that he didn't understand what was going on around him and easily forgot things. But so far, she had not seen it.

There was a crash out in the hallway or one of the nearby apartments, followed by shouting and swearing.

Despite his advanced years, Moushoom was immediately on his feet, his eyes wild, looking toward the disturbance. In his hand was the knife that only moments before had been on the TV table for them to spread butter and jam on the bannock.

"Moushoom!" Christina looked frightened by his reaction and rose as well, crashing into the TV table and nearly knocking it over.

Moushoom turned toward her, the knife held up in a defensive stance. Margie steadied the table.

"Sit down, Christina," she said quietly.

"But—" Christina looked at her Moushoom and then toward the noise in the hall. She looked terrified.

"Just sit down. You're safe. But you're frightening him more."

Christina looked at her mother for a minute, black brows

drawn down in confusion. Then she obeyed, lowering herself slowly to her seat.

Moushoom wavered. He looked at Christina, then at Margie. His eyes, though still quick, were different from the way they had been. He was separated from them by time. How far in the past he was, she didn't know, but she would give him however long he needed to calm down and make his way back to them.

"You are safe," she told Moushoom. "I don't know what is going on out there, but I don't think it is any danger to you."

Moushoom's stance gradually relaxed. He put the knife back down with the bannock with a self-deprecating laugh. "Who wants some jam?" He sat down again in his chair with a deep sigh, as if at the end of a long, physically arduous day.

"Did it scare you?" Christina said tentatively.

Margie wouldn't have tried to question Moushoom about his reaction, but she didn't stop Christina. If Moushoom didn't want to talk about it, he could say so; Margie didn't want to stop Christina and imply that it was a forbidden topic or that Moushoom was not free to share whatever he pleased.

"I am an old man. Old men scare easily."

"Why did it scare you?" Christina's eyes were on the knife. Old men might scare easily but, in Christina's experience, they didn't take up weapons to defend themselves.

"You do not know all the things that happened when I was a boy," Moushoom said slowly. "We don't talk about it." He looked at Margie. "Not all of it. We don't want to relive those years." He was silent for a few moments. "But make no mistake… we were at war with our captors. It was a silent war. But we were still warriors."

CHAPTER TWELVE

Margie's sleep was restless, interrupted by dreams that were fleeting, sliding away from her as soon as she tried to remember and analyze them. She tossed and turned, got up and had a drink of milk in the hopes that it would help her to settle down, and lay down to sleep again.

The alarm rang too early in the morning. Margie forced herself to swing her feet over the edge of the bed and to get up and get moving. Once she had been up for a little while, once she had showered and had a cup of coffee, it would be easier. Even if she were short on sleep, she would still be able to function and make it through the day.

She listened to make sure that Christina got up when her alarm rang. She let Christina choose her own wake-up time and routine, as long as it got her to school on time. Christina was old enough to be responsible for those details herself. And she had shown herself to be responsible. Most of the time. They had both found it difficult to settle down after the long visit with Moushoom. Margie's brain had been busy with all of the things they had talked about.

"I'm up," Christina croaked from her room. She knew that Margie would be close by, checking in.

"Do you want me to put bread in the toaster for you?"

"Um… yeah," Christina agreed. They both knew that food was one of the things that was sure to get her out of bed.

Their morning preparations were slow and involved their bumping into each other and into other things a lot that day. But despite their fatigue, neither was grumpy and irritable. It was just kind of a slow-motion morning. Margie saw Christina off to the bus and hopped in her car.

❧

A LOT of the high schools only had a half day on Friday. Christina would be arriving home by one o'clock, and Margie wasn't sure what she would be doing in the time until Margie returned home. Doing her homework early so that she wouldn't have to worry about it all weekend? Margie suppressed a smile. Doubtful.

She wondered if Abdul, too, would only have a half day. His father had been home when they had visited before. Margie wasn't sure what kind of a job he had, whether it required him to work on shift, or whether he could work remotely from home. Would Sadiq be watching for Abdul to come home? He didn't seem like the kind of father who supervised his son closely. He came from a culture where the children were probably allowed to run around the village barefoot all day, as long as they didn't have to be at school, work, or doing chores. Of course, that was just what Margie thought after seeing commercials about giving aid to emergency relief in the African countries. Or the occasional telethon or news report on happenings around the world from them. She didn't really know anything about the Sudan personally.

She took a break from the mind-numbing work of eliminating or prioritizing each suspect to do a quick Google search of the Sudan to learn what she should probably already know about their culture and history.

CHAPTER THIRTEEN

Margie sat with her eyes closed for a long time.

She didn't want to believe it.

She sat there, thinking things through, going through all of the variables in her mind, putting the pieces together. The picture they formed was complete, but it wasn't what she wanted to see.

She looked around the squad room to see who else was there. She'd been working with her head down for so long that she had missed the comings and goings of the other detectives. Cruz was leaning back in his chair, rubbing the back of his neck. Clearly, he had been working too long at his computer as well.

"Detective Cruz, do you want to go for a ride?"

He nodded, rolling his shoulders and continuing to rub his neck. "Yeah. Anything to get away from this desk. What do you need?"

"I think… I need to talk to Abdul James again."

He studied her face. "Abdul. I thought you had decided he wasn't a suspect. Too young and shy. Wouldn't have any motive."

"I know. I had decided that. He didn't seem like a danger. And yet…" She thought about Moushoom the night before, grabbing the table knife. Nobody would expect a frail old man to be a danger either. But he had reacted in an instant, ready to defend himself.

"You think he might be the doer, or you think he knows something?"

She wasn't ready to float her theory yet. It was too soon. She wanted some verification first. She needed more information. "Let's go over there. See if we can find anything else."

He nodded his acceptance of this plan and didn't insist that she tell him all of her thoughts. Margie agreed to go in Cruz's car. He knew his way around the city better and she wouldn't have to demonstrate her complete lack of a sense of direction. They put on their masks before sliding into the enclosed space. Cruz didn't even use his GPS when she gave him the address, but pulled out into traffic and headed toward the community.

Margie watched out the windshield, trying to memorize everything she could about the layout of the city. "Have you lived in Calgary long?"

"Fifteen years now. Four with homicide."

She was not surprised he had been there so long. He seemed to be comfortable with the culture in Calgary. He didn't sound or act like a new immigrant. And he obviously had to have the years behind him in a Canadian police force to have earned the position of detective. He couldn't do that straight off the plane.

"Do you like it?"

"Calgary or homicide?"

"I meant Calgary, but either."

"It suits me. Other than the weather. I still find it cold. The summers are nice, but they are short."

"Yes. Same with Winnipeg."

"How long did you live in Winnipeg?"

"I've been in Manitoba my whole life. Winnipeg… since high school."

"And before that?"

"A Métis community you've probably never heard of. But I wanted to get an education. There wasn't much available if I stayed home. I always figured I would go back after I finished school, but then… there's the problem of finding a suitable job. And I wouldn't have been able to find something there. Not in law enforcement."

"Have you always wanted to be in law enforcement?"

"No, not really. I kind of gravitated toward it during college. I thought I might have an aptitude for it."

He nodded and didn't express his opinion one way or the other. She hadn't worked with him long enough for him to have an opinion anyway. As long as she didn't think she was a bad detective, that was fine.

"What made you take another look at the kid?"

"Something that happened last night… and then… I couldn't stop thinking about it. I did a bit more research and thought that… I really didn't take a hard enough look the first time. I didn't get the full picture."

"You think he had motive?"

"Not exactly."

"We're going to need motive."

"Maybe."

Cruz found the street without directions. Margie wondered if he had looked it up before. Maybe he had suspected the kid and had wanted to know where he lived. How feasible it was that he had walked to the park regularly. Maybe looking for gang associations in the area.

Margie led the way to the door. She again rapped hard, demanding attention. Sadiq might not be so happy to see her again. He might want to just ignore the knock at the door and pretend he didn't hear it. Margie was impatient. "Mr. Paul!" She hammered on the door again. "I want to talk with you."

Sadiq opened the door. His dark eyes took her in, then went to Cruz, standing casually behind her, one hand in his pocket.

"What is it? I thought we were finished."

"I need to talk to you and Abdul again. Is he home?"

"No."

"Will he be home soon?"

He looked around, frowning. "Yes. It is Friday. He will be home very soon."

"We'd like to come in to talk to you."

He reluctantly opened the door and ushered them in again. Margie looked around, experiencing again the starkness of the room, the warmth of the traditional objects that made it a home, however bare it was.

"You said that you and Abdul are from the Sudan."

"Yes."

"Are you his father? His biological father?"

"No."

Margie looked at Cruz. It meant nothing to him yet, but it would.

"How did you come to be Abdul's guardian?"

Sadiq sat down on one of the chairs. "Things in my country are very bad. Terrible things happen there."

"There is a lot of war and unrest."

"Yes."

"And Abdul was orphaned?"

There was another hesitation. "Yes. Perhaps. It is hard to be sure. People disappear or are relocated. Families are broken up. They don't always know what happened to each other. Abdul lost his parents."

"How did he lose them?"

"Families get separated. His mother and sister were killed. His father... I don't know. He fought. He could not stay in his village."

Cruz turned his head suddenly and Margie realized that, once again, Abdul had slipped into the room and was standing there silently, without her even being aware of his entrance.

"Abdul. Come in. Sit down with your... guardian. We were just talking about you. About what happened in the Sudan."

He pulled down his bandana but not his hood, looking at each of them anxiously. He moved around them to sit down with

Sadiq, looking only slightly comforted by being close to someone familiar.

"When your mother was killed and your father was fighting, what did you do? Who took care of you?"

Abdul didn't answer immediately. He stared straight ahead, unmoving. He didn't fidget. He just sat there like a statue.

"I had no one," he said finally. "Many children die. They sleep in the streets. Forage. No one takes care of them."

Margie nodded encouragingly. "Is that what you did?"

"At first. I didn't know where to go or what to do. But then I found out about the battalion. The Children's Battalion."

Margie's heart beat harder. It was awful to think of what had happened to Abdul. Even though she didn't know the whole story yet, her heart went out to him. She imagined Christina or another of the many children in her extended family orphaned in a war zone.

"In the Children's Battalion, they would feed you," Abdul explained. "Three times a day! As much food as you needed. We had bunks in the barracks while they were training us. We had clothing."

"How old were you when you joined them?"

"I was ten. Not old enough to fight yet. I carried messages, acted as a spy. We had a network passing the information back to our commanders."

Margie looked at Sadiq. He had made no attempt to stop Abdul from talking about what had happened.

"How did you come to be Abdul's guardian?"

"Abdul was rescued by UNICEF and the UN. They put him through reeducation. Counseling. And they brought him and some of the other... refugees here. I wanted to help. I said I would take a child."

"Were you a child soldier as well?"

Sadiq shook his head slowly. "My mother was. She was abducted and became one of their wives. She was fifteen when I was born, and escaped. She tried to return to her village, but she was shunned as a spy and a used woman. I grew up on the streets and in orphanages until someone sponsored me to come here."

Margie swallowed. The story was told without emotion. Not something Sadiq was outraged about. Just the story of his life. How he had come to be there.

It was a fact of life in the Sudan. He and Abdul had both suffered loss and privation at an early age. It had affected them, caused changes to their brains. Maybe long-lasting. Maybe permanent.

She looked back at Abdul.

"You said that at ten, you were too young to fight. Did you become a fighter before you were rescued?"

Abdul stared down at his hands. "Yes."

"You were forced to fight?" She thought of the pictures she had seen on the internet. Children cradling submachine guns. Empty eyes. Blank faces.

"They did not force me," Abdul disagreed. "It was… what we were there to do. We had to defend our country. Our honor. It was our duty. We were glad to do it."

"You killed people."

"In a war, people die," he said flatly.

"I know… but in most wars, children are not recruited to do the killing."

He shrugged. "That is the way it was where I come from."

Margie moved on. Abdul was not responsible for what he had done in the Sudan. They put a gun in his hands and trained him to use it. Even if he had joined the battalion voluntarily, he was not the one who was responsible for those deaths. The adults who recruited and trained him were the ones at fault.

"Do you like it here in Canada?"

He smiled, showing teeth. "Oh, yes. It is a beautiful country. And no war."

"You like school?"

"Yes."

Margie looked at Sadiq. She wondered if he would stop her. It didn't seem like he would. He didn't know what the laws were in Canada or how to react like a typical Canadian parent.

"Do you get scared?" she asked Abdul.

Abdul considered the question. He nodded slowly, looking down at his hands. "Sometimes."

"I was with my grandfather yesterday. When there was a big bang and people yelling, he grabbed a knife from the table. When he was a child, he was often beaten. I don't know what else happened to him. But he was afraid. He grabbed the closest thing he could use as a weapon to protect himself."

"That is good," Abdul said with a nod. "You must protect yourself. Even an old man."

"Or a child?"

"Yes."

"Do you carry a knife to protect yourself?"

"Yes."

He turned his head, looking at her with those guileless, open eyes. Why would he feel guilty for carrying a knife? Why would he think it was wrong? He had been trained. He knew he had to protect himself. For most of his life, no one else had protected him.

"Can I see it, please?"

Abdul reached into the large pocket of his hoodie and drew it out. Not just a jackknife like she might find at a department store or Scout shop. It caught the light as he held it out to her.

A folding combat knife.

Just like a soldier would carry.

CHAPTER FOURTEEN

Margie quickly pulled a glove on over her hand and took the knife from Abdul. She didn't open it. She already knew everything she needed to. It fit the description of the kind of blade that had killed Robinson. Even if he had cleaned it well, it might still have microscopic spots of blood left on it, perhaps in the hinge. Cruz provided an evidence bag and Margie slid the knife into it.

"How did Mr. Robinson scare you?" she asked Abdul softly.

"I was walking in the trees. It helps me, walking where there are lots of trees. Alone, away from all of the people. I like Calgary, where I can live close to the park."

Margie made an encouraging noise.

"He grabbed me and yelled at me. I didn't know what he was going to do, why he was attacking me. I was just walking in the trees." Abdul blinked a few times, thinking back. Replaying it in his mind. "I don't know what happened. He did not have a weapon. I thought he would have a gun." He shook his head, trying to make sense of it. "But he died. He fell on the ground."

"Did you try to help him? To stop the bleeding?"

"No."

"Did you try to talk to anyone else? To get the police or ambulance here to help him?"

"No."

"You should have."

"I didn't want them to find me. I didn't know if there were others—soldiers who had guns. I went back home. No one followed me. I went to bed."

"Did you tell Sadiq what had happened?"

"No."

Sadiq shook his head to confirm the point. "I did not know."

"Did you know he carried a knife?"

"No."

"Abdul, you're going to need to come with us."

Abdul looked down at the floor, sighing. "Am I going to prison?"

Margie's eyes were hot, and there was a lump in her throat as she helped Abdul to his feet and closed cuffs over his stick-thin wrists. "I don't know what's going to happen, Abdul. We're going to tell the authorities what happened. If it was up to me..." Margie trailed off.

What would she do if it were up to her?

What was the appropriate consequence for what Abdul had done?

How could they do him justice and still protect others from him?

CHAPTER FIFTEEN

Margie and Cruz relayed the developments to the rest of the team, gathered together in the briefing room.

"Robinson was probably telling him to stay on the pathway or to follow some other real or assumed park rule," Margie suggested. "Abdul doesn't even know what he said. Just that Robinson grabbed him and was yelling at him for something. I guess… he had a flashback or reacted instinctively, and before he knew what he had done, Robinson was dead on the ground."

"He's got to be a psychopath," Jones said, shaking her head. "I was there when you talked to him the first time. I heard him say that nothing out of the ordinary happened at the park that night. I saw his eyes… there were no tells. Nothing to indicate that he was lying or avoiding anything."

"I think… he didn't act guilty because he doesn't feel guilty about it," Margie said uncomfortably. "Not because he's a psychopath, but because that's how he's been trained and conditioned. He lived in an environment where he had to kill or be killed. Sadiq said he went through retraining, but clearly he hasn't made the transition. Whether he ever can or not, I don't know, but he doesn't live in our world. A world where you expect to get through the day without any violence, without someone attacking or trying to kill you. Robinson attacked, he defended himself, and he survived. That makes it a good day."

"He's not going to get off of murder charges because he has a troubled past," Cruz said. "He's going to go away, and they're not going to let him out for a long time."

Margie knew Canada's laws, though. At fourteen, it was highly unlikely Abdul would be sentenced as an adult. Especially not without any kind of connection to Robinson or evidence of premeditation. For a young person, the maximum sentence for first-degree murder was ten years, and for manslaughter was likely to be far less. The judge would recommend a rehabilitation program before he would be reintegrated into his community.

That was humane and wasn't designed to punish him, but to help him. But he had already been through a rehabilitation program when he had been rescued from the Children's Battalion. Would Canada's efforts be any more effective in helping him to become a normal, contributing member of society and no longer a threat to others?

All too soon, he would be back at school with other children, walking free on the streets and trails again. Was there hope that he would understand the seriousness of taking a life in Canadian society and no longer be a threat to anyone else?

She closed her eyes and said a prayer in her head for Abdul. And for those he would touch in the future.

Over coffee, he read the article in the online paper one more time, studying Detective Marguerite Patenaude's picture in the paper and rereading the few sentences that described the homicide Detective Pat was credited with solving. There were few details because of the involvement of a young offender who, of course, could not be named or identified. But there was enough there for him to understand what had happened.

Within days of moving into Calgary, Detective Pat had already solved her first murder. She thought she was so smart. She thought that she, as an affirmative action hire, could just waltz in and show everybody up.

He put his mug in the sink and filled it with water. Then he got into his car and drove to the house where Detective Pat lived with her teenage daughter. He parked across the street and gazed at the house. She had no idea what it was like to be him. She thought she lived in his world now, but she didn't. She could turn around and go right back where she had come from.

He had plans for their Detective Pat.

He would see how she handled the next case.

FISH CREEK PROVINCIAL PARK

Fish Creek Provincial Park was established in the Fish Creek valley in southern Calgary in 1975 and is the second largest urban park in Canada, featuring over 100 km of trails for walking, running, and biking.

It offers Sikome lake, a man-made lake, for swimming. Boating and fishing is permitted on the Bow River and Fish Creek. There is an environmental learning center, a visitor center, aquatic center, and day use picnicking areas.

Most of the park remains in its natural forested state.

The Friends of Fish Creek Provincial Park Society is a non-profit, volunteer-run organization which helps to provide visitor services and many essential functions around the park.

AUTHOR NOTE

The last residential school in Canada closed its doors in 1996. The effects of the abuses perpetrated in these prisons impacted thousands and continues to affect the Indigenous community today.

On May 27, 2021, the Tk'emlups te Secwepemc First Nation announced the discovery of unmarked graves containing 215 children who had been residents of the Kamloops Indian Residential School using ground-penetrating radar. This was not an isolated incident, but part of a larger genocide that took place all across Canada. Other discoveries have been made and the tragic histories of the 139 residential schools that operated in Canada need to be exposed.

The Truth and Reconciliation Commission's final report in 2012 made specific calls to action with regard to missing children and burial information which have not been honored.

How the government of Canada responds to this discovery and makes good on their many promises made to Indigenous peoples remains to be seen.

I have been concerned for a number of years about the intergenerational trauma caused by residential schools, living conditions on reservations, and discrimination faced by the Indigenous peoples in this land, and have written about some of these issues previously in *Questing for a Dream*. It is my hope that my writing can raise awareness and educate readers on both the history and the current conditions of those who have lived these experiences.

If you are also concerned about these harms, I would encourage you to write to your MP (if you are Canadian), encouraging the federal government to follow through on the calls to action made by the Truth and Reconciliation Commission and the promises they have previously made with regard to such things as clean water, medical care, and keeping Indigenous families together.

You can also make a donation to a charity that benefits residential school survivors, such as the Indian Residential School Survivors Society.

In the Sudan and many other countries in the world, children are recruited to fight in wars and rebellions. UNICEF, United Nations, and others are working hard to put an end to these practices and to rescue and re-educate children who have been harmed by this practice. Many children have been rehabilitated and live happy, productive lives away from the wars.

For a first-person account of what it is like to be a child soldier, I recommend reading *A Long Way Gone,* the account of Ishmael Beah's experience in Sierra Leone.

Did you enjoy this book? Reviews and recommendations are vital to making a book successful.

Please leave a review at your favorite book store or review site and share it with your friends.

Don't miss the following bonus material:
Sign up for mailing list to get a free ebook
Read a sneak preview chapter
Other books by P.D. Workman
Learn more about the author

Sign up for my mailing list at pdworkman.com
and get Gluten-Free Murder for free!

PREVIEW OF LONG CLIMB TO THE TOP

CHAPTER 1

Margie Patenaude didn't need to be a detective to know who had left the dirty dishes in the sink.

"Christina!"

"Gotta go, Mom," Christina said, rushing into the room. She swept her long black hair out of the way as she shouldered her backpack so that it would not get caught under the strap. "The bus will be here any second. I'll see you after school." She headed toward the front door. "Oh, and you remember what I told you, right, about the Métis Club meeting after school today? So I'll be late. Don't expect me right after school."

"You left dishes in the sink—"

"I have to go. If I stop and do them now, I'll miss the bus, and then you'll need to drive me to school." Christina had the door open and was halfway out. "Sorry. I'll load the dishwasher tonight. Okay? Bye!"

Margie watched her fifteen-year-old race across the street to the bus stop. And she was right, of course; the bus was making its way down the street, and if she had taken an extra ten seconds to have a conversation or rinse off the dishes, she would have missed it. But that was no excuse for Christina to leave them in the sink in the first place, when she knew she was supposed to rinse them and put them directly into the dishwasher.

She sighed and did it herself. She had to drive into work, and the other homicide detectives and Sergeant MacDonald wouldn't know whether she had left five minutes later because of her daughter or if she had just hit the lights wrong or run into a traffic snarl on Blackfoot Trail. She checked the table and counter for any other orphaned dishes and didn't find any. In another minute, she had the dishwasher running, Stella was settled for the day, and Margie was walking at a quick clip out to her car. It was a cool, crisp morning.

"Oh, Detective Pat!" called Mrs. Rose, a sweet little old lady who was the first and only owner of the 1960s bungalow next to Margie's.

Margie stopped, anxious to get on her way but not willing to be rude or pretend that she hadn't heard Mrs. Rose's call. She took a couple of steps toward her neighbor, but stopped the prescribed two meters away. "Yes, Mrs. Rose? What can I do for you?"

"I just wanted to make sure that you had heard that the 55+ Society is open again."

Margie's expression must have betrayed her consternation at this announcement. Mrs. Rose smiled her sweet, pink-lipstick smile. "The 55+ Society. It's over there on Twenty-Sixth Avenue, where your grandfather lives."

"Oh, yes…?"

"And it's been closed since the whole pandemic thing. But they've opened up again. And they have lots of programs for the seniors in the area. You should take a look at the activities and clubs that they run, see if there is anything that your grandfather would like to go to."

"Oh! Okay, I will," Margie agreed. She would see if there were anything that might interest Moushoom. "Thank you for letting me know."

"They probably have flyers in the lobby of the building he lives in. But if they don't, the 55+ Society is just about a block away. You can stop in there any time they are open and get their program guide. And they can give you a tour. They're very helpful over there."

"That's great. I'm glad you let me know." Margie gave Mrs. Rose a firm nod, then turned back toward her car. "Have a wonderful day."

"I will, dear. You too."

THE WORKDAY PASSED QUICKLY. The homicide team was working on a number of open cases, but none of them was burning hot. It was a matter of chasing down leads one at a time. Doing background checks on persons of interest, interviewing them, looking for connections or alibis. The day-to-day work of a homicide department.

She found it easier to move from one case to another than to stay focused on one all day, so she gathered shorter tasks from the primary investigator on each of the cases, read the file to bring herself up to speed, and worked on her assignment. Then she would jump to the next case.

No one on the team seemed to mind her ADHD approach. They were happy to have some of the less-desirable tasks taken off of their hands. Margie was eyeing the clock, trying to decide whether she would have time to review one more case before leaving for the day when Sergeant MacDonald—Mac—walked up to her desk. He was a tall man, towering over her when she was sitting down. His hair was almost entirely silver and he had lines of 'experience' around his mouth. He readjusted his thin-rimmed glasses.

"Yes, sir?" Margie immediately tried to think of what she might have done to attract his attention. Good or bad, she didn't want to be under the sergeant's scrutiny too often. Too much praise from him and the rest of the team would resent her, and too much criticism… well, any criticism was likely to keep Margie up half the night with anxiety over her mistake and how to avoid making it again in the future. No one liked being criticized, and Margie felt that she was particularly thin-skinned about it. She criticized herself for not accepting criticism well. How was that for a fault?

"I've got a case for you. I know you like to be home when your daughter gets home from school, but this one is going to need your immediate attention."

The duty room was still as everyone else listened in. Margie had just solved the Fish Creek Park murder case. The next case should have gone to someone else. Although everyone else already had active files and Margie did not, so maybe that was why he had picked her.

"Uh, yes sir. She's going to be later today and, of course, when it's urgent, I can take the time I need to get started on it. She's old enough to be on her own for a few hours if I'm needed elsewhere."

She didn't ask him what he had for her but, of course, that was the question on the minds of everyone in the room.

Mac nodded his appreciation. He ran his fingers through his short gray hair and leaned on her desk. "Here's the thing. It's the same MO as the Fish Creek Park murder."

Margie's eyes went wide. She stared at him in surprise. "The same MO?"

Robinson had been killed with a single stab wound. Margie had caught the killer. So they knew that it wasn't the same killer. Just because another person was killed by a stab wound, that didn't make it the same killer or the same case.

"The same MO," MacDonald agreed. "It's another provincial park. Male victim. Single stab wound with a single-edged blade. Bled out. No apparent provocation, no one heard yelling or was aware that anything was wrong. Body discovered by a family walking the trail with a toddler in a stroller."

Not a dog-walker this time. But Margie was sure there were probably a number of dog-walkers close by. That one difference didn't make the case different from the Fish Creek murder.

She hoped that the toddler hadn't seen anything and wasn't old enough to remember it later. Hopefully, she had been sleeping peacefully in the stroller at the time. It was a good time for an afternoon nap.

"Okay. I'll look up this park and go see," Margie agreed. "Is it near Fish Creek Park?"

"No. Halfway to Cochrane. It's actually outside of Calgary city limits, but we are heading it up because of the connection to the Fish Creek case. Since it looks like the same killer."

"It's not, though," Margie pointed out.

"There's always the possibility that we got the wrong person for the Fish Creek murder."

"But he admitted to it. We didn't get the wrong person."

"I don't think so either. But innocent people do confess. It's also possible that he was released on bail or under his foster father's supervision and is no longer in custody."

"But if this other park isn't close to his home… how would he get there? He couldn't walk there like he did to Fish Creek. Is there a bus that goes all the way out there?"

"No, I don't think there's any bus service out there. Tours maybe. I'm sure it's not related. But because of the similarity in the cases and the sites of the homicide, it's your case."

"Okay. Give me the details." Margie looked at her watch. If she remembered correctly, Cochrane was west, toward the mountains. Margie's home was in the east, on the opposite side of the city. She was going to be more than an hour or two late getting home for Christina. Just the travel time would add an extra hour, forget any investigative work and waiting for someone from the medical examiner's office.

"Glenbow Ranch Provincial Park," Sergeant MacDonald told her. He spelled it out for her. "Do you want directions?"

"Will it be on my GPS? If it's outside of the city, it might not be…"

"Should be. It opened in 2011, so it's been there long enough".

ॐ

Long Climb to the Top is book 2 in the *Parks Pat Mysteries* series and can be ordered at pdworkman.com

ABOUT THE AUTHOR

Award-winning and USA Today bestselling author P.D. (Pamela) Workman writes riveting mystery/suspense and young adult books dealing with mental illness, addiction, abuse, and other real-life issues. For as long as she can remember, the blank page has held an incredible allure and from a very young age she was trying to write her own books.

Workman wrote her first complete novel at the age of twelve and continued to write as a hobby for many years. She started publishing in 2013. She has won several literary awards from Library Services for Youth in Custody for her young adult fiction. She currently has over 60 published titles and can be found at pdworkman.com.

Born and raised in Alberta, Workman has been married for over 25 years and has one son.

Please visit P.D. Workman at pdworkman.com to see what else she is working on, to join her mailing list, and to link to her social networks.

If you enjoyed this book, please take the time to recommend it to other purchasers with a review or star rating and share it with your friends!

facebook.com/pdworkmanauthor
twitter.com/pdworkmanauthor
instagram.com/pdworkmanauthor
amazon.com/author/pdworkman
bookbub.com/authors/p-d-workman
goodreads.com/pdworkman
linkedin.com/in/pdworkman
pinterest.com/pdworkmanauthor
youtube.com/pdworkman

www.ingramcontent.com/pod-product-compliance
Lightning Source LLC
Chambersburg PA
CBHW030818200726
48288CB00004B/1286